'Rebel inc. score again with the debut collection of ten short stories from the great Laura Hird . . . Buy it.'
iD Magazine

'With cutting insights and sharp style . . . Librarians should file with care.'
The Face

'If you're a fan of the Scottish blend of realism, this short story collection is one for you . . . A sense of irretrievable loss – of compassion, innocence, love – drives the best of these short stories.'
The Herald

'A genuinely interesting writer.'
The Scotsman

'[This] first collection confirms the flowering of a wonderfully versatile imagination on the literary horizon – and one unafraid of a few thistles and creepy crawlies . . . There is fine pacing to the dramas, and careful crafting that is not ostentatious. But the keynotes here are wit and energy: sharp and steady – right on the nail.'
Independent on Sunday

Nail and other stories

Laura Hird

First published in 1997 by Rebel inc.,
an imprint of Canongate Books Ltd,
14 High Street, Edinburgh EH1 1TE

This edition first published in 1999

Rebel inc. series editor: Kevin Williamson

'The Hard Sell' appeared in *Verbal*, 1995; 'Of Cats and Women'
appeared in *Cencrastus*, 1995; 'Imaginary Friends' appeared in
Chapman, 1996.

The Publishers gratefully acknowledge subsidy from the Scottish
Arts Council towards the publication of the volume.

British Library Cataloguing-in-Publication Data

A catalogue record for this book is available upon request
from the British Library

ISBN 0 86241 850 X

Typeset by Palimpsest Book Production Limited,
Polmont, Stirlingshire
Printed and bound by Caledonian International Book
Manufacturing, Bishopbriggs, Glasgow

Contents

For Ecky Plum

Nail

AT FIRST I thought it was a spale. There was just this little ink line on the index finger nail of my right hand. I tried pulling on it with a pair of tweezers then picked at it with a match sharpened by my teeth. All to no avail. As it started to protrude from the nail, I constantly poked and agitated it until it overhung my finger by about 2mm. It looked like a tiny twig made out of blackened skin. The growth also continued under the nail where it had branched out into two roots both disappearing into the half moon of my cuticle. It was as if some kind of bug or eel had burrowed under my skin.

Although it appeared to consist of a fleshy fibre it had no sensation. At first I would nibble tentatively at its tip, afraid to fully sink my teeth into it for fear it was a malignant mole of some sort and I would haemorrhage. But eventually I grew so irritated by the uninvited guest that I bit the end off it. Although it bled quite heavily I felt nothing, which reinforced my sense that this thing was not part of me but something separate which had made my body its home.

Eventually, having grown increasingly distraught about the whole thing, I made an appointment with the doctor then cancelled at the last moment. Fear of what was causing my affliction superseded the fear of what it could do to me. I racked my brains for what could have caused it. What had I been eating around the time I'd first noticed it? Where had I been? Anything out of the ordinary. But I came up blank.

As self-consciousness about my condition grew more acute I started avoiding people to avert the possibility of anyone having a cheap laugh at my expense. There were several people whom I knew would find it hilarious. I've always taken great pride in my hands and nails, you see, always been terribly fussy about them. My fingers are long, slender and artistic, like a pianist's, and I'm often complimented on them. Due to this I am fastidious about their upkeep – moisturising them, being extra-careful the soap I use doesn't dry the skin in any way, keeping the nails at a finely manicured quarter of an inch which I tend daily with nail strengthener, filing them as unconsciously as others bite theirs, keeping the skin far back on the cuticles, carefully varnishing them with Yves Saint Laurent ivory nail polish so they never look painted, just healthy and strong.

Even as a child I was acutely aware of my hands. This was intensified by the revulsion I used to feel at my sister, Helen, who would bite her nails down to the knuckle, peeling the surrounding skin down with her teeth until the end of each finger was just a festering, scabby mess. Those fingers used to give me nightmares. They disgusted me and in turn my sister did, and always has, disgusted me.

If I used bottom-of-the-range, chain-store treatments I could understand but I always buy the best. The only remotely feasible explanation I can come up with is that something has crawled into my Nailon when the lid was off and somehow became embedded in my nail. You'll understand now why I'm reluctant to go to the doctor. Surely the implication would be that I live in the sort of squalor Helen seems to relish, which I most certainly don't. My house, like my person, is immaculate.

By the end of the first week the appendage has protruded by about 5mm and fattened up. The bitten-off part has healed and now looks as if it may sprout a second branch. Panicking again, I try another home remedy to rid myself of this deformity. I burn the tip over a lighter until it chars and lets off a smell like pork chops on a barbecue. Again there is no pain but the messages of discomfort and disgust are like those induced by the drill at the dentist – the edginess and nausea that a local anaesthetic can't curtail. A drop of lava-like matter drips onto the newspaper and I have to stop because I feel so sick. Also, although I am managing to eradicate the tip, I would have to burn off my finger to kill the roots.

On waking the next day I notice a new, pink, fleshy bud has appeared in the centre of the blackened ball on my finger. I have stopped answering the phone and put a message on the machine saying I'm away for a few days. All I can think about is this monstrosity growing out my nail. I telephone Helen and give her abuse, picturing her disgusting, red-raw fingers as I try to organise her ridiculous life, resenting her more than I ever have.

By the following day the bud has sprouted a few more millimetres and has a bloom the size of a match head. As I bang my hand off the tallboy to punish it I ponder that I would rather have no hand at all than this. I must try something else. Bringing out my sewing box I loop a piece of black thread round the shoot, pull it down to the shank then close the knot around it. The thread disappears into the flesh of the thing and becomes so tightly ingrained I can't pull it free. Trying to pick it loose with a pin, I pierce and bloody the thing as I go but cannot even find the thread. I gag as I stab blindly at it then realise, with disgust, that I haven't even sterilised the needle. A fortnight ago the idea of placing anything in my person that had not first been sterilised would have horrified me. Deformity is no excuse for dropping standards, however I've probably given myself blood poisoning by now so I continue assaulting it. Eventually the thread begins to loosen and I pull it free with bits of mutated carcass attached to it. I spray *Paris* on the wound in an attempt to dry it out. Still I feel no pain whatsoever.

In growing desperation I decide to go to the library to see if I can find any mention of a similar affliction. The parking there is hopeless so I pull on my black leather gloves and camel coat and start to walk. It is a blisteringly hot day and everybody I pass seems to be smirking at my inappropriate attire, but I push myself onwards. The fresh air and space feel alien after the past few days.

Striding across the Meadows, I veer in the opposite direction when anyone approaches me which elongates my journey somewhat but I just keep going. As I pass the dirty black hulk of the Infirmary I briefly consider going along to dermatology and insisting on seeing someone but I'm honestly not ready for that yet. I need an idea of what it might be before I decide whether I'm prepared to share it with anyone else.

The shops I usually stop in to exercise my Visa card are bypassed, Napiers the Herbalist being the first. Perhaps if I find a suitable prognosis at the library I can pop in on my way back. They needn't know it's for me, although the gloves could be a giveaway. Then I try to ignore the enticing buy-me buy-me sweep of designer shops in Candlemaker Row, the Deutsche Gramophone CD sale in Bauermeister's and the book about Morningside in the window I've been meaning to buy for months. I have never not yielded to such temptation before. This must be serious.

With one squeaky sweep of its heavy door I am inside Central Library and breathing its reassuringly musty smell. The small reference-only section in the main library are just to my left as I push through the next door. It is virtually deserted in there, just a few bespectacled twenty somethings in long raincoats furtively loitering around the French literature and philosophy sections. The librarian is across at the other side of the room putting books back onto their shelves, the sound of her movements muffled.

I run my glove over the spines of the medical reference books before she comes back to the desk – aromatherapy, reflexology, cancer care, diet books, exercise books, books about coping with grief. Just as I hear the trolley squeaking back over towards me I spot it, the silent consultant, *The Complete Guide to Symptoms and Illness*. Pulling it free, I place it face down on the table beside me. As I instinctively begin to take off my coat I suddenly realise how foolish I'll look sitting just in my gloves, pretend I was just looking for something in the pocket, and sit down.

The librarian is back at her desk now. She looks over, gives me a can-I-help-you smile and I give her a thanks-but-no-thanks one back and begin flicking through the telephone directory of text. In here, on one of these pages is the answer, I am confident.

I skim through the book from cover to cover. Consulting the index is pointless since I have no idea what I'm supposed to be looking for anyway. It's all in here though, dozens of possibilities. I check the definitions at the top of each page, stopping at any that sound remotely similar – boils, cellulitis, dyshidrosis (blisters on the fingertips apparently, too small though). Erythema nodosum sounds promising, 6cm nodules, but then I notice it is an affliction of the legs. Folliculitis only results in pustules. This is surely way beyond the pustule stage. Grunuloma annulare with domed papules. What is a papule? Then I notice something about ring-shaped lesions, so they're out the window as well. Hookworm or roundworm infection causes tunnel-like lesions that grow a centimetre every day it says, but again they seem limited to legs or buttocks. Skipping past lice, unable to even look at the page, next up is molluscum contagiosum, which is these damned papules again, 3mm this time, then I see the words 'DNA virus of the pox group' and again have to turn the page. Raynaud's phenomenon sounds severe enough and apparently causes chronic infections in the nails so I write the name down in my diary then notice the words 'possible amputation'. Surely not? I study it further. It seems to affect women between twenty and forty-five, me, but only the latter part of the symptoms apply. No harm in having the name anyway. Paronychia sounds horrific but seems to be nothing more than tender fingernails that ooze pus. Oh for the simplicity of tender fingernails that oozed pus. The closest I can to find to my own problem is a sebaceous cyst but they only seem to happen in hairy places. Perhaps there are tiny hairs under your fingernails, they're everywhere else. After reading that they can be cut off, however, I feel slightly less concerned about my earlier, primitive attempts at amputation. Or how about sporotrichosis, nodules under the skin of your fingers caused by something in soil. I shouldn't think so. I never touch dirt. Then I'm at warts and I'm no further forward. None of these things really seems apt, unless I've picked up some fatal leg disease in my nail. I doubt it.

My eyes briefly scan the shelf again although if it is indeed a medical problem I would have expected it to be in a book that has everything from grit in your eye to San Jaoquin Valley Fever.

Putting the book back on the shelf, I thank the librarian, stop the first taxi I see outside and ask to be taken home. If anything I feel worse now. Do I have athlete's foot in my finger or some foul venereal-sounding ailment? Or is it something different and unworldly? When we get to the house I throw five pounds at the driver, feverishly unlock the door then double-lock the world out again.

Throwing the gloves off before I even reach the living room I prepare for the worst. Oh God, it's grown another couple of millimetres, I know it has. The exposed twiggy part was shorter than the actual nail when I went out, now it's definitely longer. I'm not imagining it, I'm more than definite. Retrieving the discarded gloves from the hall carpet, I put them in the kitchen bin for fear the infection has now wormed its way into the leather. They were my favourites as well, not wildly expensive but moulded to my slender fingers and extremely comfortable. This is wretched. As I instinctively reach for the espresso machine, however, I find myself unable to touch it. I rescue the offending glove from the bin and put it on again.

The desire for a coffee has vanished, it'll only speed up my heart and make me worse. Instead I throw myself on the settee, almost hoping I'll break it and give myself an excuse to get in a rage and let off some steam. It remains stolidly intact though so instead I sit sulking and grinding my teeth to chalk-dust until my heartbeat has accelerated naturally and my gloved hand is starting to perspire. I can't stand this, I can't stand just waiting around for it to get worse. If there's no improvement by tomorrow I have to call the doctor, I must do something.

Switching on the television, desperate to scribble over my line of thought I channel-hop mindlessly for a while then read a line from my latest Maeve Binchy several times and still don't know what it says. The house is absolutely filthy. If I were invited to a house in a state like this I'd make an excuse to leave. All I have the motivation to do is scowl at it and let it add to my misery. I could phone Helen again but I don't think I can even work up the enthusiasm to chastise her. My life seems monotonous, like it has always been monotonous. The expectedness of it starts to niggle me, despite the presence of something that completely defies rational explanation living on my skin.

Attempting a gin and tonic, the first sip transports me so far from my present situation that it gives me vertigo to contemplate it and I have to pour the drink away. The television is turned on-off-on-off-on-off-on-off. This is hopeless, I want this time passed and the next part to begin. Why can't you fast-forward your life past these commercial breaks of despair? I decide to do just that, force myself through to the medicine cabinet and swallow down a couple of Temazepams. The idea of giving up on a day at 5.30 galls me but I just can't bear to be awake any longer.

Switching on the electric blanket to hasten my unconsciousness I stand behind a chink in the curtain watching pigeons in the garden. I hope the black tom cat that makes this his territory is watching too as I do find it exciting when he catches them, the nonchalant brutality of it. There's nothing strange about these feelings, though, it's just like watching a wildlife documentary out your window. But there is no sign of him today and the vermin are safe to peck their fat little heads stupid over a half-eaten pizza. There is a bin directly opposite my gate so why someone chose to deposit their midnight snack in my garden is anyone's guess. People are disgusting, no wonder there's so much disease.

The debris on the lawn recalls the terrible mess the house is in and I look at the clouds to avoid thinking about it. I watch two vapour trails growing across the sky, one behind the other, and puzzle over how they manage not to crash. Then I notice another, over to the left, expanding much faster than the other two. I try to work out how far they are from each other in an attempt to explain why the solitary one seems to be going at twice the speed of the others. Perhaps it's a flying saucer. For all I know half the vapour trails I see could be flying saucers. Why do people go hunting for these things at night, as if massive, glaring objects that look nothing like anything we put up in the sky would choose to observe us when they would be most conspicuous? In daytime, far enough away from Earth, they could look quite ordinary. Why am I thinking these ridiculous thoughts? Daytime alien crafts that drop viruses into our atmosphere when we least expect it? Who's to say though? This is daft. The pills must be starting to work. Pulling the curtains over the galaxy I strip, snuggle into the gloriously warm bed and switch off the electric blanket. The heat soon evaporates my otherworldly concerns.

I wake early, 6.45, feeling positive and clearheaded. The respite is brief, however, evaporating as soon as I become conscious of my still wearing the glove. I make a coffee and take it over to the settee with me before peeling my hand free. I do a double take and check my other hand, thinking I must have them mixed up somehow. By the light of the window I study the finger, not able to accept that the thing has disappeared. Not even a hint of where it once was. Carefully turning the glove inside-out I check the relevant finger-hole, nothing. Sitting down, I scrutinise my hand for some tiny shred of evidence that the growth ever existed. The nail looks exactly as it had before this happened.

A queasy feeling of unreality stalks me all morning and I suspect I may even still be asleep. Each time I lose sight of my hand for more than a minute I have to study it afterwards to check the thing's not returned. There is no feeling of relief because I am not convinced it has truly gone.

Life prior to this seems light-years away, I can't even really remember what it was like. If I had the routine of work to lull me back to normality it might help but my next contract doesn't start for two months. Money's not a problem, they pay me so ridiculously well, but I just need something to get my head into.

As the morning progresses the desire to get out and start putting it all behind me intensifies. At the moment every room in the house reminds me of my recently departed deformity and I know I'll need to do something normal before I can break this feeling. Lunch at Raffaelli's with my friend Jenny then a few hours' frantic activity with my Jenners card might do the trick. But by the time I call, her machine is switched on and she's off having a life somewhere.

However, I still have this overwhelming need to get out of here for a while and have the company of another human being, anyone at all. I'm not used to isolation like this. There's always my damned sister of course but that really does stink of desperation. Helen is a Mary Erskine girl like myself but shows no signs of the fortune my parents spent on her education. Craigroyston would have probably suited her better. The thought of being seen in Raffaelli's with that though is out of the question. Pierre Victoire's is rather tacky but probably a safer bet. These places are usually crawling with scruffy arty-types in the afternoons so she won't look so out of place.

The sorry creature is beside herself when I call and doesn't mention the mouthful I gave her the last time we spoke. Why does she always have to be so bloody nice? I often wonder if she has a personality at all or if she is purely reactive. If she just let rip occasionally I probably wouldn't pick on her so much. I'm just trying to toughen her up a bit.

I pull the cellophane off my last consignment from the Fraser's sale, a beautiful olive Alexon suit. To hell with dressing down for Helen's benefit, I could go in wearing a postal sack and still make her look dowdy.

Once I've showered, applied a liberal amount of makeup and painted my nails for the first time in ages I begin to feel more like my old self. Pulling on the suit and adding a few finishing touches I'm on the verge of breaking into a smile. The fact that I've conquered something so terrifying on my own and can emerge looking this good is actually quite inspiring.

I'm still trying to decide whether to confide in Helen about it all when I enter Pierre Victoire's and see her already sitting at a table in her Bosnian refugee coat. Standing up to greet me, she begins pawing me like a poodle after a titbit.

'Oh Charlotte, it's so nice to see you. It's super you phoned, I really feel like a good old chat.'

'You are planning to stay then?' I ask, glaring at the mottled tweed rug, expecting moths to appear.

Shuffling her upholstery onto the back of the chair she stares enthusiastically about at the tacky mock-Gallic décor as I sit cringing.

'Golly, this is posh. It's like *A Year in Provence* in here, don't you think?'

'They do a fairly decent lunch for under a fiver so I thought it might be up your street.'

As I study the wine list she announces that she just wants a coke because she doesn't like drinking in the afternoon. I insist on wine, however, as I simply refuse to order a soft drink for anyone over the age of ten.

Her face flushes instantaneously as she takes the first sip. Then she refuses to order, insisting I choose for her because she doesn't understand what the things on the menu are.

'Don't be ridiculous, pick something.'

'What do you recommend?'

'I don't know, I can't remember what you like. It's fairly self-explanatory for God's sake, mussels, see, you know what those are, soup, you know what that is, melon, what exactly is it you don't understand?'

Why does she persist in putting on this retarded child act when we're out in public together?

'OK then, big sister. What about the mussels, are they nice? And maybe the cod, I think I know what that is, and sticky toffee pudding, I can just imagine what that is. Sounds gorgeous, have you had that before?'

'As I said. It's only a fiver but it's edible.'

What was I thinking of? Helen's voluptuous enthusiasm about everything is causing my shoulders to tense up and ache. As she takes a few more sips of wine the adolescent flush on her face spreads up over her ears and her eyes are watering away with the joy of my asking her out for lunch. Jesus, she seems squiffy already. I hate flirtatious women like her who pretend to be helplessly drunk after half a glass of wine.

Suddenly, as if to reaffirm my previous thought she stands up and does a little twirl in the middle of the restaurant, arms outstretched.

'What do you think?'

'Of what? Sit down for God's sake.'

Ignoring me, she remains standing there like a mannequin.

'This, it's a Marks and Sparks, what do you think? Smashing, isn't it? How much do you think it was?'

'I don't have a clue. I only go there for food and underwear.'

'Oh come on, have a guess, what do you think?' and then she starts twirling again and I know I'll have to take a guess to get her to sit down.

'Forty pounds?' I whisper, knowing full well Helen would never spend that on a dress, not even her wedding dress.

'Three pounds fifty in Barnardo's. It's never been worn, look, see the label, it's brand new.'

Then she's pulling the label out the neckline and straining across the table so I can see it. I'm having difficulty trying to recall a more humiliating time but I have to humour her before she'll sit down, then continue to do so for fear she'll get up again. Can we possibly have the same genes?

Then she starts going on about Rosemary, her little girl. I wondered how long it would take. About all the tests she's been having and being too scared to sleep in case she snuffs it during the night and her passing out at school, every tiny detail. I've heard it all so many times before. She knows I hate children but she still keeps going on about it. Most annoying, however, is the fact that the child's ill-health allows her this celebrity-like status amongst everyone we know. It seems like it's the only thing our family has talked about for the past six years. Surely it's wrong to treat the child differently just because she's ill? But no, if anyone else has a problem these days they're meant to count their blessings because they've already had lives and Rosemary's is almost over. It's not that I'm insensitive but I sometimes wish she would just die and be done with it so we could all get back to normal.

Nananana nananana nananana on and on in my ear. The conversation is always the same. If I wrote it down before we met I'd probably have it word for word. One of the main reasons I taunt her the way I do is to try and trick her into forming a whole new sentence.

Trying to block the noise out by listening to myself chew I watch her trying aimlessly to liberate the mussels from their shells, praying that no one I know will come in and catch me with this ineptitude. It's no good though, I can still hear her. In a desperate bid to end the death's-door stuff before I slap her, I guide her onto her only other topic of conversation.

'How's Kevin? Working at the moment?'

Kevin, how could one of our family possibly marry someone called Kevin? I refuse to say his name when I'm discussing her with people, it's just so embarrassing. He went to Portobello High School for God's sake. Delighted that I've shown a bit of interest, she launches into another ramble.

'Oh, the contract out at Riccarton finished at the end of June. It's all temporary contract things these days. It causes terrible friction between Kevin and his pals because they're all competing for the same few jobs. He's doing a bit of delivery work at the moment just to get away from all the back-stabbing, it was really getting him down. The money's not great but he's a lot happier.'

He's always been a selfish bastard.

'Why didn't you marry that Brian Millar bloke? He's

lecturing at St Andrews now. Wasn't he after you for a while?'

'The one with the terrible acne who used to break wind in class?' she starts giggling inanely '. . . Windy Millar, you surely don't mean Windy Millar?'

'He'd have been a good catch for you. Surely flatulence and bad skin have to be better than what you ended up with?'

That wipes the smile off her face.

'What?'

'Well, come on, you're hardly in a position to feel superior about it, are you, after the tiddler you ended up with. He's hardly Donald Trump is he?'

Ooh, she almost looks annoyed.

'Look, Brian Millar was an absolute creep. I happen to love Kevin, in case you'd forgotten. I don't bother about money the way you do, I just want to be happy.'

That's about the most excitable I've ever seen her, I must be doing some good. Why does she always have to make allowances for that runt though? Her life would be so much better if she'd never met him. Even the Rosemary thing, I'm sure was genetic. You can't just breed with anything. Weak men like him never stick around for long anyway. He'll be off and it'll be up to mother and me to pick up the pieces, as if mother's well enough to worry about something like that.

'I don't know, Helen, sometimes I think you just married him to get at mum.'

Oh, the bottom lip's away. Is that all it's going to take this time? She really is so impossibly hittable, her weakness infuriates me so much. She pushes away her mutilated mussels, finishing them is obviously too complex for her. The clatter of her cutlery reverberates throughout the restaurant.

'Why are you like this, Charlotte? Why did you phone me? Sometimes I think you don't even like me. Kevin likes you, you don't even know what he's like.'

Oh yes I do. I know what he was like last new year. Bastard. I never felt like killing myself as much as I did the morning after that. Not so much the fact he'd knocked me back but the fact I'd tried in the first place. With that piece of shit.

By the time the waitress clears away our starter dishes and serves the main course, thoughts of her awful husband have ruined both our appetites. I look at her stupidly sad face staring down at her cod and her disgusting nails, albeit not as disgusting as they used to be (even Kevin must have his limits).

'You have to eat it after the struggle you had choosing it.'

'Honestly, Charlotte, I'll leave if you carry on like this. Why are you being so nasty? I've got enough on my plate as it is.'

She misses the irony of her own words, naturally.

'. . . have I ever criticised anything you've done? I'd always support you, whatever you did.'

'Oh don't start the last-of-the-Christian-martyrs bit, please. It just seems like nobody's entitled to an opinion anymore unless they have a sick child. I have problems too you know, like you wouldn't imagine, my health is pretty bad too but I wouldn't dream of burdening you with it. Things I don't deserve. At least you know where all your problems stem from and you can do something about it.'

For a moment I think the waterworks are finally starting but instead she slaps a ten-pound note on the table and struggles into her rug again.

'I really don't want to fall out with you again, Charlotte. I'm sorry but I just don't need this.'

With a waft of *L'Aimant* and a Wagnerian rumble of tables she's gone and I'm left fidgeting with my Dover sole, too ashamed to look up and see if anyone's watching. I could die. When the waitress notices the neglected plates I grab my bag, pay at the door then get the hell out of there.

My car is reached in a blur. I have to batter at the steering wheel for a while to release some of the anger before my vision starts to clear. Squinting at my finger it still looks OK but somewhere at the back of my brain I see flashing spots and just want to get back to the house before I have a full-scale migraine. By the time I get to my door, zig-zags are attacking my brain and my legs are buckling under me from the pressure in my skull.

I manage to swallow four Nurofen Ultra, a couple of Temazepam and get my frozen Zorro mask from the freezer before kicking my shoes off and collapsing onto the bed. The shock of the icy mask and snakes of chill running past my temples numb me as I squeeze my eyes shut and let out a wail of temporary relief.

The heavy dark-blue velvet curtains are shut and the room is just a blackened impression of itself but the Glenlivet firework display is banging around my head. Lying here I wonder what I've done to deserve this. Helen's no doubt run home to Kevin and told him what an insensitive monster I am. Why is everyone so scared to hear the truth about themselves? Surely it's better to be honest with people than to let them keep making the same mistakes over and over again? Everyone acknowledges it's essential to do it with children so why does all this don't-want-to-hurt-their-feelings nonsense start when you become an adult? There's none of that when

I'm working abroad, I just tell people what to do and they do it. Things could not function properly otherwise. Perhaps it's just the bloody Scots and that stupid resentment they have for anyone who does well. People who work hard terrify them. That's why I only get these hellish migraines when I'm here.

I must sleep, it's the only thing that will shift this. The lights are dying down but I can feel the pain coming, like a drill in my temple, pulling the life out of the right side of my face. Rolling around on the bed I try to find a position that gives me some kind of relief but the movement just makes it worse. Eventually I can stand it no longer and decide that stomach down, face in the pillow is probably the most comfortable but still the pain is so intense it would kill your average man. Fumbling the duvet out from under me I manage to cover my legs but I'm too weak with this aching drowsiness to sort the thing properly. Each time I exhale I tell a different part of my body to relax, from my toes slowly upwards, listening to my breath falling against the pillow. Please let me sleep, please let me sleep. Willing the painkillers to disperse I try to imagine them sending clouds of healing fluid to my head. Surely they must have started working by now? The lights have completely gone and I'm just aware of the deep red roundness of my closed eyelids. Putting my good ear to the pillow I listen to my blood pumping, it sometimes helps me to sleep, the solitude is glorious. Pushing my hands under the pillow, I pad the sides of my head in the warmth of it.

Somewhere in the distance a telephone starts ringing, each ring louder than the last until I realise it's mine. Dammit. I try to ignore it but it persists 10 . . . 11 . . . 12 . . . 13 . . . 14 times, they must be keen . . . 16 . . . 17 . . . 18, oh no, what horrific thing has happened now? 20 . . . 21 . . . 22. I struggle through to the living room, supporting myself with an invisible rail of furniture, imagining my father lying beside the lawnmower with blue lips or that mother's been raped by someone on community care. With great effort I lift the receiver to my ear. It's bloody Kevin, I don't believe it.

'What have you been saying to Helen? She's greetin' her eyes out through there. Why do you always have to pick on her? What has she done to upset you so much?'

Replying would require more effort than this is worthy of.

'. . . please Charlotte, if you dinnae mind I'd prefer if you didnae phone her till you've sorted yourself out. She really doesnae deserve it. Did she tell you . . .'

Throwing the phone down I tell it to piss off. What a bloody nerve. Telling me when I can and can't speak to my own sister. It starts ringing again almost immediately so I pull it out the wall and decide to leave it like that for the foreseeable future. Play them at their own game.

Swallowing another couple of Nurofen and one more Temazepam I check my finger in case the stress has brought on a relapse. I'm almost surprised that it's still fine considering the downward spiral my life is taking. Any relief I might feel is subdued by the phone call. The slight lull in my headache is no more than a tea-break. They always have a slight recess to allow themselves to get second wind.

If I can just get to sleep before it gets too ferocious. Retiring again to the darkened bedroom the whole process of warming up the bed has to be repeated as the phone call has eradicated all trace of heat. I'm too tired now to risk putting the electric blanket on again as my mind has already started issuing nonsensical signals of its imminent retiral.

The migraine is on a crescendo again as I waft into a wave of gibberish about radiators talking to each other. I listen to the minutes click down on my radio alarm till 8.13 when the day finally drifts out of my reach.

I am in a familiar city that I have travelled to many times before, a city built from lots of different places I've been condensed into one, everything with a new but familiar location. The street in Corstorphine where I was brought up has an East Finchley Greek grocer's and an Enfield street corner. We are on the coast, North Berwick beach straddled by the steep enclave up to the ruin of St Anthony's. An open boat-hut from the Union Canal is where the ruin should be, filled with waltzer carriages from the shows. I know this city as well as I know any of the places it includes, its structure never changes. It looks like Eastern Europe but I am repeatedly told it is on the west coast of America. The hotel I find myself booking into is a cross between Notre Dame and St Pancras station, its masonry blackened like St Mary's. Although alone I have arranged to meet my mother and Helen and a friend of theirs. The reception area is the bank in Hanover Street with black iron antiquated lift cages from the Royal Infirmary. There are no porters and as I search for my room I soon become lost in the labyrinth of stairways and long arterial corridors which house the hotel's 813 rooms. Although the place seems deserted, there is a revolution going on below in the street. This city has always been at war, only the factions change, but I always find myself just out of harm's way, on the periphery, sometimes protected by nothing other than a hedge but still completely safe. Black leather gloves cover the charred stumps where my fingers used to be, however deformities of this kind are the norm here. The war has touched everybody's life. As I watch below

I see crowds suddenly exploding into blackened chunks of flesh, or mown down by firing squads, bodies jumbled into shapeless mounds as tanks roll over them. Each time I glimpse from one of the hotel's many windows I witness the deaths of at least a dozen people. Knowing I am safe though, the carnage does not upset me in any way, I am merely irritated that I cannot find my room. Hours seem to pass as I run along the corridors, stopping every now and then to spectate on the slaughter below. As each corridor looks the same and none of the doors are numbered I begin checking each room individually. The décor in each is identical – stark, grey, musty with a large damp patch between the cornice and window frame. Many rooms are empty apart from a single bed, sink and metal-framed khaki canvas chair, always in the same position. The vantage point from every window is also the same, however each one supersedes the last in extremes of visible violence. In other rooms there are silent families or solitary businessmen sitting by the windows eating packets of cheap biscuits. My presence is never noticed. In another room I find mother looking like David Bowie but this seems completely normal. Father and her sit playing Scrabble. His lips are blue but I can't remember when I last saw him looking so healthy. Though we exchange no words my look adequately explains that I am still locating my own room. She points next door where I find Phil, a friend of my old flame, Bob, with whom we spent our only ever weekend together. He leans beside the window which, unlike the others, has yellow, ochre-coloured curtains which emphasise his unhealthy pallor. His skin was probably this colour the last time we met (he was having tests on his liver) but I didn't notice it then. Without prompting, he tells me that he died three years ago but, again, this seems reasonable and I ask him if he has seen Bob recently, how Bob is, what Bob's doing, if he can send me a copy of the photo he took of Bob and me before we went to that wedding, the only real proof we were ever together. Suddenly overwhelmed I burst into tears, Phil holds me and all I can think of is that photo, and how I felt that day, when Bob was all mine for that one weekend. I desperately want that photo, not just to prove to myself that we were together once but to see if it captured the desire we felt for each other for that short time. Phil disturbs my thought and points down to the street just as an oriental-looking General draws his sword across the throats of three young soldiers who are tied to a lamppost. The cacophony of firing squads and land mines exploding choreographs the scene but all I can think of is this damned photograph of Bob and me. When I turn to Phil again I notice thick wiry hair hanging from his nostrils which disgusts me so much I have to shake him free and run from the room to continue my search. At the end of this corridor is a large arch-shaped window which I feel as if I am being pulled towards. As I draw nearer and nearer to it I hear Vaughan Williams' Variations on a Theme of Thomas Tallis. It gets louder as I approach, an incredible feeling of anticipation washing over me. With my next step I feel the clammy heat of the duvet around me. The pillow is cradling my head. I remember having dreamt about that place again, and that Phil was there. Why did I dream about Phil after all that time? The bed feels emptier than it has for years. Variations on a Theme of Thomas Tallis is playing on the radio alarm, the opening bars.

Yesterday starts to flood over me again as I rise, put a little water and some ground Swazi coffee into the espresso machine and switch on the gas. My finger is clear but I am still greatly affected by it. Today I must start phoning people and putting my life back together. It's as if I'm getting over a very long illness. I must take control before it takes control of me.

Switching on the mindless burr of Richard and Judy I go through to the bathroom and turn on the shower. Maybe the water will lash me into some sort of coherence again. As I lean down to put a towel on the floor I sense something on the end of my nose, like a piece of stranded tissue. I wipe at it with the sleeve of my nightdress but it doesn't move. Touching it I feel a hard lump just under the nostril, like a scab or something. As I run my finger down it though I realise it is pointed. Squeaking the condensation off the mirror I put my face up against it. It feels as if someone has punched me in the stomach, taken all the air out of me. A brownish lump hangs from my nose like a raisin. I tentatively put my finger up the nostril to check it isn't just some kind of bed bug crawled up my nose through the night. It is rooted there though, about halfway up. A piercing pain prevents me pulling on it. I'm about to cry but I try to stop myself or I won't be able to see it.

Grabbing the magnifying mirror from the bedside table I go through to the living room and switch the overhead lamp on. Oh Jesus no, not another one, not on my face, please. Pulling the mirror back for a better look I stare at the grotesque bogey, much fatter and sturdier than that which recently adorned my nail. I study my face from several angles. From each it is glaringly apparent, the sort of thing that nothing could really disguise other than immediate conversion to Islam. Trying to push it back up induces the pain of several papercuts and I have to stop. The coffee is gurgling in panic through in the kitchen but I don't really care any more if the whole bloody house goes up in flames.

What is happening to me? Am I dying from some strange

unworldly cancer? If my existence continues on this bleak path I almost hope that is so. Though I know I'm being extremely foolish I still can't bring myself to call the doctor, have my worst fears confirmed or exceeded, and the incredible embarrassment, I just can't. Why didn't I go private years ago, that wouldn't be quite so bad. Somewhere like the Murrayfield I could bear but what if they rush me into the Infirmary with a ward full of snoring, chain-smoking old fishwives and a gang of giggling students coming round to laugh at me once a day? My reluctance to phone the practice is not helped by the knowledge that the sister of one of my friends works on the reception desk and we're forever being regaled with news of who's got the clap, who's impotent, who's having a nervous breakdown. It's hilarious when it's someone else.

What finally shifted the thing in my nail? Did it just vanish overnight? Though I try desperately to remember what I was doing the night before last, my mind is completely blank. I suppose that I must have phoned Helen but that is merely speculation. The last few days are a blur, I can't even remember when this started. Is the pressure of having to deal with something like this on my own making me doo-lally?

If there was somebody who cared about me, I could confide in them but the truth is I trust no one, not even mother, not that she's malicious just that she simply can't keep her mouth shut. Surely there must be a helpline for things like this, problems you're too ashamed to go to the doctor about? I pull the directory from under the phone and start thumbing through the community services numbers at the front. There's six organisations to deal with maltreated animals right at the start so there must be something for people like me. The racial equality people, I notice they get two entries.

Community health, here it is – blood donation, dental emergency service, family planning, sexually transmitted diseases clinic, this is ridiculous. Thousands of pounds' worth of wasted resources for the self-inflicted problems of weak people who've probably never paid a penny of income tax – alcohol and drug abuse, eight numbers; marriage counselling, two numbers; oh look, divorced and separated, another two numbers; single parents, two; women's aid, four. If those people just had a shred of morality or self-control in the first place all that money could be used on people who are genuinely ill. Nothing looks remotely apt. If I'd gone out dressed like a tramp and someone had raped me I'd be fine, or if I was an overeater or just out of prison, for crying out loud. What do I try now? I don't even know what I need – a herbalist, an exorcist, a wart surgeon? In faint hope I look up the word nose in the alphabetical index. I don't believe it, one entry, Nose to Tail Pet Care, Innerwick. As I lob the Thomson directory across the room I knock half a cupful of coffee left from the other night onto the carpet. My reflexes throw me into the kitchen for a basin of hot soapy water then I'm kneeling on the floor scrubbing at the grotty smell of day-old coffee and Axminster, crying at the utter wretchedness of it all. I never cry. The fact that I left the drink on the carpet in the first place confirms for me that my standards are dropping. A month ago I'd have reprimanded anyone who left a cup in such a stupid place, now look at me. No matter how much I scrub at the offending stain, the awful stink of coffee remains and I can smell the milk getting sourer by the second. Feeling the thing lurking there when I sniff I sense it is growing. Going to the bathroom for a closer look, a billow of steam hits me as I open the door and I can barely see to switch the shower off, let alone study the tumour. My God the house is an absolute pit. It's like Helen's place, absolutely filthy. No wonder I've got things growing out of me, I'm probably crawling in bacteria.

Falling to my knees I gag bile into the toilet bowl. The sense of squalor is tangible and I can almost feel it creeping over me. An intense need to be cleansed overwhelms me and I pull off my nightdress and step under the shower. It scalds into my body like a tattoo but I stand there defiantly, bearing it, hoping that the high temperature will burn whatever it is away. There is reassurance in this pain because at least it has a rationale. Putting my face up to the steaming spray I let the water scorch into my nostrils. Choking, I can almost feel the water coming out my ears but I persevere, determined to be done with it, to drown it. I continue firing the jet up into my head, practically asphyxiating myself until a stream of blood rolls down my hand and begins dripping off my wrist into the bath. Nauseated I gag again then almost collapse, breaking my fall on the toilet cistern. Blood now plops onto the toilet seat and tiled floor. Dizzily stuffing a handful of toilet roll to my face to stem the flow I pull the towel round me and stagger through to the living room to see if my masochism has felled the growth in any way. I'm praying that the blood is coming from it, that it's dying. All I can see when I enter the room though is the huge stain still there on the carpet and the basin of foul-smelling water. I want to run out in the street and leave it, run away from all of this. I can't bear to touch it again.

The makeshift toilet-paper dressing has disintegrated into a burgundy piece of string. Jamming a tissue up each nostril I pick up the basin, carry it out through the kitchen and throw it into the garden, locking the door behind it as if it might come running back in again. All my hatred is directed towards that basin as I suddenly feel that it could be silently responsible for all this.

Still the smell of coffee pervades the entire house. It's not until I pick the Temazepam up from where I left them on the kitchen bunker though that I notice the silver espresso maker is now black and rat-tat-tatting frantically to be rescued from the gas. I turn it off, grab the charred pot with a tea towel and throw it sizzling into the sink. Who knows where the bath towel has gone? Was I naked when I threw the basin into the garden? I'm going senile, spilling things everywhere, forgetting where I've put things, leaving the gas and shower on, going out in the nude. Who is this person I've become, I don't recognise myself. Perhaps the monster is taking over my entire being, growing inside me as well as out.

In the short time since I awoke my life has completely collapsed around me. The real Charlotte has been abducted and replaced with something awful. I'm sure it was the old me in the dream last night but now I am gone. Why did I wake up thinking about that bloody man this morning? He wasn't even in the dream, was he? Already the day has gone on too long. I'm not well enough to have to contemplate this kind of horror.

As I swallow down two sleeping tablets with a glass of milk I realise that even this insignificant act is totally out of character. The last time I drank milk straight like this was in the days before I knew what cellulite was. I can almost feel the fat congealing on my body as the pills go down. At last, I think, a normal thought.

The flow of blood is abating slightly by now so I check my face to see what may have evolved since I last looked. Both nostrils are caked with blood, the thing just lying there in the middle looking almost as if it is pulsing. On closer inspection

I realise that I imagined this but it is still absolutely grotesque, like a nicotine-stained maggot just hanging there. How could it grow so quickly? Did I touch my nose and pass it from my finger? Surely if that were the case I would be covered in them by now?

Again, thoughts of ringing the doctor are soon erased by the possibility of my new, extremely contagious disease ending up on the front page of the *Times* with a photo of me with that thing hanging out my nose. Please don't let me end up as some living specimen, known for nothing other than my deformity.

Surveying once more the disarray that was once my living room it smells as if the aroma of burned coffee is oozing out of my every pour. Clothes, towels, phone books, dirty cups seem to have taken over my living space, dust lies thick on the furniture and my bare feet keep treading on sore, hard lumps in the carpet. If I hadn't taken those pills I would gut the place out but although I've been awake less than an hour I'm already completely fatigued again.

The desire to go back to sleep is starting to evaporate however as I'd rather keep watch over my appendage in case it starts growing again.

Switching the television back on I try to watch a talk show about teenagers who weigh more than twenty stone. It's disgusting. Everyone is feigning sympathy but really they should wire their disgusting jaws up or stick a pin in them. How could anyone let themselves get in a state like that? Much as I try to distract myself with these terminally ugly creatures it is not easy to keep my mind off my nose. Just thinking about it is making me boss-eyed. What if it never goes away and I can never let anyone see me again?

Oh no, I'm starting to drop off and my nose hasn't stopped

bleeding. I'll choke on my own blood, though that would probably be a good thing. Sleep only makes it worse, I have to fight it. Sitting steadfastly on the settee trying to ward off waves of tiredness I realise I am fighting a losing battle. Did I take two Temazapams or four? Dabs of blood flourish on the ocean of blue tissue making it a purple map of the world.

My eyes close and it feels good. With part of me trying to convince the other to just submit, I have to force myself upright. As I try to find potential saviours in the phone book again it feels incredibly heavy and my vision is so blurred I can barely make out the photos, let alone the tiny letters. Before long I am once again basking behind the safety of my shut eyelids until the voices on the television are just a calming drone. Calm, calm, calm I whisper each time I exhale. Then I'm aware of a rustling noise in front of me. As I direct my hearing I think I hear a voice whisper, 'she's gone', but when I try to focus through my droopy eyelids there is no one there, just the hellish blemish. Oh but I feel so relaxed now. The traffic sounds lovely.

I wake up in the foetal position on the settee, perspiring underneath my thick bath robe. From the comfort of the sticky heat I can still sense it there touching my upper lip but I lie for a while not wanting to spoil the safe ignorance of uncertainty. Obese people are still flickering on the TV screen but the clock says 1415. Then I see that fat Jewish woman presenter and realise this must be a different load of obese people. Is this what I'm destined for, guest appearances on daytime TV with studio audiences with a joint IQ of fifty gasping at my affliction and the Marje Proops-type woman that does the cooking with tears in her eyes at my plight? It's no good, I have to check it.

Knocking the mirror onto the floor I have to fumble on

the filthy carpet for it, my ineptitude giving me a stab of further misery. By the light of the window I look but feel nothing because I have started to expect the worst anyway. What a idiot I was not to phone the doctor earlier. The thing has fattened and is at least a centimetre longer, like a small prune. Touching it sends a shooting pain right down my spine but in the slight contact I feel lumps on its hide. Enduring the sting I seek out its root to ensure it is still confined to my nostril. There is that to be thankful for at least.

This has gone on long enough, I have to phone the doctor. The survival instinct has surpassed my other fears. They can't force me into hospital if I don't want to go, I just have to know what it is. It's so long since I needed to call the doctor I have to get the number from my address book.

When I ask for a house call the receptionist asks what the problem is.

'Sorry, I'd rather not say.'

'I'm afraid the doctor's finished doing house calls for today. I need to know what the problem is if you require an emergency call.'

'I can't tell you but it definitely is an emergency, I assure you.'

'I'm sorry madam, I can't authorise an emergency call unless you tell me what the problem is.'

How much do I pay in national insurance contributions for this?

'I can't tell you because I don't know. Please, I need to see a doctor as soon as possible.'

'There'll be three doctors on this evening. There's no appointments until next Wednesday but if you'd like to come in at five for the emergency surgery someone would see you eventually.'

'I need a doctor to come to me. I think it may be contagious.'

She sound bored by it all, as if she wants away for her break.

'Can I ask the doctor to phone you?'

'You can if you wish but ultimately I will need to see someone. Something terrible is happening to me.'

'It would be so much easier if you could give me some details. . .'

'But. . .'

'. . . however, I'll see if someone can call round. You'll have to wait a while though.'

'That's fine. Just make sure the doctor comes, please.'

Why didn't I hand in a box of Quality Street for the receptionists at Xmas? Mother's been doing that for years to butter them up, not that they deserve it, but she can always get seen at a moment's notice. The relief of knowing that I'm soon going to be able to unburden myself makes my not phoning earlier seem even more ridiculous.

Gently washing my face with warm water, in case soap should irritate the thing, I scrape the dried blood away with a cloth. Every time I touch the thing I get that same jolt of pain. As I dry myself I peruse the now slug-like eruption. Perhaps I should just get a pair of scissors and cut it off. The root is so far up my nostril it would be impossible though. My face looks like that of someone fifteen years older than me but I'm scared to put any make up on. Perhaps if I'd cleansed my face properly last night this might not have happened. Taking the face cloth and towel I've just used I put them in a bin bag on their own and tie it tightly shut. Who knows how long the infection can last outwith the body?

Pulling the hearth rug over the damp patch in the living

room I spray *Paris* round the room to disguise the smell. Then I put on the rubber gloves and mop up the mess I made tumbling out the shower. Even after I've finished squaring the place up I find it impossible to take the Viyellas off as it feels like they are protecting me in some way.

As long as I keep active I can fight off the fatigue. Pottering around, I try to make the place look a bit more respectable. Each time I pass a mirror though I stand prodding myself for about ten minutes till I forget what it was I was doing. Much as I try to put the house back to normal, something is not quite right. The living room may look more like its old self but I don't recognise it as mine. To pass time quicker I try to watch TV again but the glow of the screen emphasises the mollusc in my vision and I soon give up.

By 5.30 I'm having second thoughts about having phoned the doctor. I can't get this picture out my head of me lying under a large see-through tent in the middle of a ward full of empty-gummed geriatrics with severe flatulence problems. If they try to put me in hospital I'll lock myself in the bathroom and swallow a bottle of paracetamol, I swear. Imagine having no control over who visited me and all these horrors from my past turning up to gloat. In a bid to keep my nerve I try to balance these thoughts with the possibility of waking up tomorrow with a full trunk or forked tail or realising I've turned into a damned mermaid.

6.15, 6.20, 6.25 . . . what time does the surgery shut? When I call to confirm that someone is still coming, a tinny voice announces the opening times. I throw the phone down. What if she didn't take me seriously? Why didn't I take her name? Should I phone 999? I'm sure ambulances must get called out to far less serious things than this. 6.45. I decide to wait until seven before calling in the cavalry.

The thing seems to have stabilised at the size of a slug but I can't risk sleeping again. Watching the minutes tick by on the clock, at 6.56 the bell finally goes. I can't believe I'm finally going to share it with someone, that it's going to be resolved in some way.

Rushing into the hall I anticipate the shadow of the doctor through the frosted glass panels of the door but there appears to be no one there and light streams uninterrupted along the carpet. Tentatively turning the key in the lock I put my hand over my face and briefly check the garden. Nobody. How long ago did I hear it ring? Have I had a blackout of some sort?

Retreating back into the house I double-lock the world out again. Some of the local children are maybe trying to torment me. The bell goes again as I walk back up the hall. I turn round instantaneously but again there appears to be no one there. Who is doing this to me? Is this all linked in some way? It rings again as I go into the living room, this time prolonged and emphatic. Pushing the door shut I roll the armchair across the room against it though I'm not even sure why. I stand behind the curtain and watch the empty path as the ringing continues.

Imaginary Friends

MR PATERSON WAS like no other adult she'd ever met. She'd only known him for three Wednesdays but already they were the best of friends. When her last piano teacher had gone on holiday to Blackpool and not come back she hoped she wouldn't have to take lessons anymore. Now she had Mr Paterson, she practised all the time without her mother even having to tell her.

He had a lovely, big, fluffy dog called Caliban that he said she could take for walks. Her mother wouldn't let her at first but after a few days' pestering, eventually agreed. As long as she did it before tea as a girl in the year below her at school had almost been stolen by a car the other week. She'd always wanted a dog of her own but her mother said they were a nuisance and her father sneezed. Mr Paterson said she could come and see Caliban whenever she wanted because no child should be without a pet. He also gave her sweeties and fizzy juice and told her they weren't really bad for your teeth. Parents only said that to punish children.

She thought he was great. He'd play with her and not get bored, just like her best friend, Mark. Because he was an adult though, he knew what they were like – how they pretended all the things she liked were bad for her; how they said there was a bogeyman just so she couldn't play outside at night;

how they only sent her to school so they could play all day when she wasn't there.

She'd turned up for her last lesson with him crying because a big girl at school had hit her for hiding her bag in the toilets. The girl always bullied her and she thought if she stole her bag she might stop but instead she'd pulled her hair and scratched her and thrown her on the ground. Mr Paterson was all nice about it and told her she shouldn't steal anything unless she knew she wouldn't get caught. He'd given her a cuddle then they'd thrown cushions at each other until she got the hiccups. She didn't even have to play the piano. He just told her to practise extra hard and not tell her mother. Best of all he promised to show her some magic the next time she came round.

She ran to his house after school the following day. He was in the middle of giving a lesson so she took Caliban for a quick walk but was back at his door within minutes, desperate to see some magic. He laughed when he saw she was back so quickly and ruffled her hair.

'You can't wait, can you?'

He led her into the kitchen, sat her at the table with some comics and a milk shake and left her with the dog while he finished giving the lesson. She looked around at his things but didn't touch – not that he'd mind but he was still an adult. There was a photo stuck to the fridge of him with a lady and a little girl, younger than her. They all looked very happy and it made her feel a bit sad but she didn't know why.

When he came back through he saw her gazing across at the photo and pointed at it.

'That's my wife and little girl. Her name's Miranda.'

She walked over to have a closer look but the picture made her feel odd so she looked up at him instead.

'Where do they go during the day?'

He smiled and squeezed her shoulder.

'Oh, they don't live here anymore. We're divorced. They stay in England.'

Gosh, divorced! She thought only famous people and Elizabeth Taylor could afford to get divorced. At least that's what her mother always said when she'd been shouting at her dad.

'They don't stay in Blackpool, do they?'

He held her hand and his eyebrows went wavy.

'No, why? What's special about Blackpool?'

She told him about her old piano teacher going there and her mum saying she wasn't coming back. When she and mum and dad went there for their holidays she never wanted to come home but they only ever stayed for two Fridays. When her old piano teacher and her Auntie Agnes and her hamster had gone there though, she'd never seen them again. Auntie Agnes had been really ill in hospital for ages, then one day she'd gone to visit her with mum and she'd gone off to Blackpool. Why would a sick old lady want to go there?

He laughed and made her another milk shake then sat opposite and stared at her like she was a picture.

'There's a lot of magic in Blackpool. Did you know that?'

She felt all excited. He took her hand again and continued.

'Yes, in the fairground, on the pier, even in the Tower. It's a very magical place. That's why there's all those lights. They use the power from all the magic as electricity.'

It all suddenly became clear to her. She'd always known Blackpool was a special place.

'I suppose you'll be wanting to see some magic now?'

She nodded her head enthusiastically and grinned at him. He stood up and took a bottle of clear, purple liquid from the kitchen cabinet and a box of matches from the drawer.

'First we have to summon the firebird.'

She giggled, 'What the what?'

He handed her the matches, rolled up his sleeves and stood over the sink pouring the purple liquid onto his hands and arms.

'The firebird. Once you've seen it you'll be one of the secret society. You won't be able to tell.'

He poured more liquid onto himself then asked her to light a match. There was a strong smell like her grandfather's feet. She struck the match three times before it lit. He stood over it and she jumped back as his hands became engulfed in flame. He joined his thumbs and wagged his fingers as if he were making shadow pictures on the wall.

'Do you see it? Do you see it?'

She looked into the fire and gazed at his hands. His fingers were blurred by the flames but as she stared she slowly saw the firebird appear, fluttering in the middle of it all. He was almost shouting now.

'Do you see it?'

'Yes, yes, I see it,' she giggled, banging her straw into the milkshake.

He blew on his hands and the flames vanished then he pulled a face and said the F-word. He looked at her and smiled, breathless.

'I think the firebird bit me!'

He explained to her that now she'd seen the firebird and was part of the secret society, she couldn't tell anybody about it. If she breathed a word to anyone about the magic they were going to do together then the secret would be broken and he'd lose his magic powers. She swore to tell no one, indeed she felt important to be a member of the secret society and begged him to produce a rabbit or a white pigeon from somewhere. He told her he could only do one piece of magic a day during the summer or his powers would weaken. They were stronger in the winter because Jesus was born then and it was Jesus who had first invented magic. Just as Jesus had turned water into wine and raised the dead, Mr Paterson could summon the firebird.

He was sorry to disappoint her, though, and asked if some chocolate would make up for it. It was only an hour until her tea but as everything was now secret between them she sat on his knee as he scooped thick chocolate spread from a jar and they licked it off his fingers. If she was good, and didn't tell anyone, then in the winter time when his powers were strong he'd teach her how to fly. She was overjoyed. She imagined flying off into a tree when the big girl at school bullied her or her mother tried to smack her. He bounced her up and down on his knee, gave her a kiss then left her to play with Caliban and went into the toilet for ages.

Rolling about on the floor with the dog, she tickled its huge, fluffy belly, dreaming about all the things they'd do when they could fly. Then she heard funny noises coming from the bathroom. She calmed the animal down and listened. She could hear Mr Paterson breathing loudly and the occasional little moan, like he was going into a trance or something. She began to feel a bit scared in case he'd taken ill. Just as she was about to knock on the door, he came back through to the kitchen, smiling.

Holding out his hand he showed her some white stuff that looked like liquid soap and told her it was special potion. If she drank it her mother wouldn't be able to tell she'd been eating chocolate or playing with matches. He moved it closer to her face. It didn't look very nice. Like that horrible stuff on top of fried eggs that her mum said was the dead chick. She pushed his hand away, laughing, and pulled a face.

'I can rub it into your skin instead. That works just as well. Do you want me to?'

'It looks horrible.'

He sat on the settee and asked her to come and stand between his legs.

'It helps you keep secrets and it'll make you feel nice too.'

She walked over to him and he tugged her T-shirt out of her trousers with his free hand and lifted it up to just under her arms. She expected the potion to feel cold but it was just normal, and as he'd said, it did feel nice as his big hands rubbed it slowly onto her tummy and chest and back. He made her watch as it disappeared into her skin.

'See, it really is magic!'

He gave her little kisses on the back of her neck and shoulders that made her feel all tingly, and told her that this meant that the spell was completed successfully. Then he made her promise again that she wouldn't tell anybody, not only because he'd lose his powers but because if the magic got into the wrong people's hands they might use it to do bad things. She promised, thanked him several times for letting her in the secret society, and said she had to go for her tea. He kissed her on the side of the neck, gave her a magic lollipop and told her not to come round for a couple of days in case her mum got annoyed.

Although she felt sad, she smiled until he closed the door then walked home in tears. Two days seemed like the longest of times. She didn't want to leave him, or Caliban. She didn't want to go home and eat horrible vegetables and pasta then be forced to read some boring schoolbook.

Her mother smacked her when she got home and told her the next time she walked the dog she had to come home and say where she was going first. She could only eat some of her tea as she felt sick from all the chocolate and milk shakes, but her mother forced her to finish her broccoli before she left the table. Mr Paterson didn't force her to eat things she didn't want, but then again he'd never offer her something as revolting as broccoli in the first place. It occurred to her that her mother maybe found things lying in the garden and made her eat them just to be nasty.

She had to spend a whole hour on her awful project on Germany and all the horrible people who lived there, then she went next door to see her friend, Mark, and play action men with him. She wanted to tell him about the firebird and Jesus inventing magic but she was scared to. Mr Paterson might lose his powers and she wouldn't learn to fly in the winter.

She cried herself to sleep for the next two nights because she missed him so much. Why couldn't she run away with him and Caliban and be his magician's assistant and have him stick swords through her and then say, 'Only kidding!' She wanted to rescue him from a car crash then take him home and sit on his knee and kiss him.

She practised the piano especially hard so she could impress him at her next lesson. After a very long two days she went round to his house again. He was talking to another pupil's mother so he gave her the dog and told her to come back in half an hour.

Running up the street, she laughed and smiled with Caliban bounding at her side. Seeing him again had made her feel all safe and happy. Climbing through a hole in the waste-ground fence, she tied the dog's lead to a piece of rusty pipe and climbed to the top of her favourite tree. She waved down at Caliban and shouted his name. The dog pranced about, barking, pulling at its lead and wagging its tail. If only she could fly down, pick it up and take it up to sit on the tree with her. Just wait until winter. It would be just like that film about the snowman she'd seen on the telly.

When she took the dog back the lady had left. Mr Paterson looked a bit worried as he led her through to the living room. She asked him what was wrong. He sat on the settee and smiled at her.

'It's nothing. That lady was just a bit annoyed, that's all.'

How could anyone possibly be angry with him? She didn't know what to say so she knelt on the floor and started playing with the dog. Lighting a cigarette he took a deep puff. She'd never seen him smoking before but it looked nice. He looked at her, worried again.

'You haven't told anybody, have you?'

'Of course not!'

Smiling again he opened his arms.

'Don't I get a cuddle then?'

She crawled across to him and stood up. He put out his cigarette then squeezed her really tight and rubbed his nose on her neck. She stroked his hair, so glad to see him she felt like crying. She liked being cuddled. Her parents had stopped cuddling her last year. They said that seven was too old for cuddles as people might get the wrong idea. They did say the oddest things sometimes.

He eventually released her and she knelt at his feet. He played with her hair and stared at her sadly.

'Have you been thinking about me?'

She held his hand and looked back at him.

'Yes, I've been thinking about flying. I wanted to ask you about it.'

'Uh huh?'

'Well, if people see you flying, don't they know you're magic? Won't the firebird die because they'll know the secret? Won't you lose your powers?'

He told her it was all right. Before you flew you put on an invisible suit so the only people who could see you were people in the secret society.

Invisible! Think of all the things she could do if she was invisible. It got better and better. She asked him where he would get the invisible suit and he said he kept a few on top of his wardrobe. She pleaded with him to let her try one on, just for a few minutes. They wouldn't have to do any more magic today, just, please could she try one on. Just to see what it was like?

He stood up and kissed the top of the head.

'You're terrible, you know that? I shouldn't really do this until winter.'

He went into the bedroom and came back through with a suitcase that he laid on the floor in front of the settee and sat down again.

'You'll have to take your clothes off though.'

She looked up, shocked and asked him why.

'Because it only makes people invisible, not their clothes.'

She sat on the floor, not quite knowing what to do. It felt a bit strange getting undressed when her mum wasn't there but she could trust him. He wouldn't tell anybody because he'd seen the firebird too.

She began taking her clothes off slowly. He sat watching with his hands in his pockets. She stripped to her pants then hesitated and looked at him again, her face red.

'Do I have to take everything off?'

He raised his eyebrows.

'Well, people would think it a bit strange if they saw a pair of knickers flying about the sky. It's OK. I've seen it all before. I have a wee girl, remember?'

She took off her pants then stood looking at him. He smiled and gestured to her.

'Come and sit here for a minute. I want to talk to you.'

He lifted her onto his lap and began kissing her neck and shoulders and chest.

'These are magic kisses. They make sure people can see you again when you take the suit off.'

As he continued kissing her, Caliban began barking at the window. Mr Paterson looked up to see what was wrong then the doorbell rang. He stood up suddenly and she fell onto the carpet.

'Sorry, are you OK? I don't know who it is.'

She felt panicky and began picking her clothes off the floor.

'What'll I do? What about the firebird?'

He rushed her into the bathroom and told her to get dressed and not to come out until he told her. It seemed like she was in there for ages. The doorbell rang another five times, each time longer than the last, then stopped. For a while she couldn't hear any noise at all which made her feel scared. Then she felt bored. She waited and waited until finally he opened the door and peered in.

'Are you all right? I think they've gone.'

She walked out the bathroom.

'Who was it? I have to go home for my tea. Mum'll kill me.'

He walked through to the living room and sat down on

the settee without saying anything. His body was shaking so she took his hand. It felt all cold and damp and made her arm vibrate it was trembling so much. He put his other hand on her shoulder and looked into her eyes.

'I think the magic's in danger. I think the people who were at the door know about it.'

She felt frightened, imagining the belting she'd get if her mum found out. What if there was no more magic in the world and it was all her fault? What would happen to Caliban?

'But how did they find out? I didn't tell anybody.'

He didn't answer. He was thinking. Finally he looked at her again.

'I think I'll have to put the invisible suit on for a while. Until they stop looking. And Caliban too.'

She felt like she was going to cry.

'But what about me?'

'Well, if I'm invisible I can be with you all the time. Nobody'll know . . .'

He cuddled her.

'. . . as long as you remember the firebird and keep it secret.'

He told her she wouldn't even have to speak to him, just think and he could read her mind. She could finally have a dog and her mum and dad wouldn't even have to know about it. He told her he would keep the suit on until the next time she went to Blackpool then he'd come back and they could do magic on the pier and fly off the top of the Tower together. She felt it was going to be all right. All her dreams were coming true.

He wasn't shaking as much now. He went into the toilet for a little while to look for the potion then came back through and rubbed it into her so no one would know their new plan. He told her it would be better if she went out the back door in case the people who'd come for the magic were still outside.

Lifting her onto the wall between his garden and the street, he told her she was his best friend and that he and Caliban would be with her when she fell asleep then she dropped onto the pavement and ran all the way home.

By the time she turned into her road she wasn't scared any more as she sensed Mr Paterson and Caliban were already with her. When her mother smacked her she was brave and didn't cry because she knew they were watching. She spent the weekend in her room playing them all her favourite records and having silent conversations and two days later, when her mother said that one of the neighbours had told her that Mr Paterson had disappeared, she laughed in her head and heard him laughing back.

The Last Supper

I WENT ROUND to Dave's a fortnight ago to watch the Prince Naseem fight. Although I'd been avoiding him since his marriage broke up six months ago the fact of the matter is I don't have cable myself and he said on the phone his cupboard was full of Jack Daniels his brother-in-law smuggles over from Calais. It seemed like an appropriate time to finally do my dutiful friend bit.

With the fight to distract us everything was fine. We tried to inspire the deaf Mexican boxer with a mantra of racist obscenities, willing him to finally floor that arrogant little shite. Sadly, this was to no avail and with the foregone conclusion and a bottle of Jack Daniels behind us Dave started to get all maudlin. First, about Shirley moving her new man into his house. More fool him, I said, wait till the guy realises what he's been lumbered with, go round and kick the crap out the pair of them, all sound advice although I suspected Dave had probably suggested they move in together himself. He's weird like that.

Then he started to get a bit watery-eyed and told me he was now getting kicked out the bedsit. His stuff all needed moved but as he'd never bothered learning to drive himself he was overdrawn on favours with everyone after his previous flit from the marital home. Next thing he grabbed my arm and started crying into my shirt sleeve and, you know, I really hate seeing guys do that. It's second nature to women, just their way of getting what they want, but when you see a bloke doing it you know things must be pretty dire.

The drink had given me a pitying sort of affection for the guy though, so I was giving him the don't worry about it pal, I'll sort it all out, my brother's got a van, leave it to me, absolutely insist, least I can do sort of nonsense. Why do I always promise these things I don't mean when I'm pissed? You always sort of hope the people concerned will die or get a life before you have to honour drunken pledges. I hate waking up and realising I've been nice to some arsehole I can't stand the night before.

Anyway, I've spent the last fortnight trying to think of an excuse and now it's too late. Tonight is the night. Though I could most definitely do without it I can't handle the guilt of letting him down at the last minute. Also when people have something on you, you can't go upsetting them too much, know what I mean?

The flat's like a pit as well, I've been wearing the same shirt for three days because I need to do a washing and all I've eaten all day is a sausage roll about eleven this morning. At least I'm working from home tomorrow. What a waste of a fucking night, though, I feel like going out and getting bladdered. I'm still trying to think of a convincing excuse when the phone rings.

'Darren, it's Dave. Just checking you're still on for tonight, pal.'

'I said I'd do it so I'll do it, OK!'

'It's just I'm going to have to pay another day's rent if I don't get the stuff out by nine. The landlord won't check the room till I'm there. Are you sure you don't mind?'

'I'll be there, right. Like I said. Look, I've got some other things to do so I'll see you later.'

Before he has time to elaborate on his paranoid injustices of the rented sector I hang up. There's no sense in listening to his crap till it's absolutely necessary. Why do lonely people feel they have to inflict their misery on everyone else? Don't they realise that's why they're lonely in the first place?

The town's a nightmare. There's a summit on or something so the one-way system has degenerated into a no-way system. When I finally turn into his mother's street he's standing at the end of the path looking out for me. At least we can get out of here before his old dear appears. Then while I'm double-parking at his door the arsehole waves and runs back into the house and before I know it Bette Davis has hot-footed it down the hall and is knocking through the glass at me. Fuck it! I wind down the window and she's away.

'Oh Darren, what do you make of all this? What a carry on, do you think he'll be all right? He's too sensitive for his own good, even when he was wee, remember? I don't keep very good health myself, you know, I'm a bit old for all this bother. Do you think it's money? Is there another man? The doctor's got him on these pills but I don't think they're doing him much good, he just sits around all day, he's not been to see us for months, do you think I should have a word with the doctor myself? Oh Darren, will you try and cheer him up tonight? He needs a bit of male company since his dad died, will you help him? Please, for me . . .'

Assuming a fixed grin I sit nodding my head politely until finally the passenger door slams and Dave's in beside me with his hands over his eyes. I give her a smile and speed off with her shouting behind us, 'You will come round for tea though, Darren? Come round next week.'

'Sorry about that, pal, nobody should have to suffer that. I'm not going to be able to handle it there for long. I'll clock her one, I swear I will. I just keep losing it with her and then feeling guilty all the time.'

'She's bound to expect a bit of abuse, she's your old dear.'

'No man, I'm losing the place, these Prozac don't do anything, just wipe me out.'

There's an awkward silence in which he probably thinks I'm contemplating the tragedy that is his life but I'm wishing the sap would sort it out. I cut up the Southside to avoid the road blocks. If I'm going to make him buy me a pint I'll sit through enough whingeing later. Apparently his uncle's moved most of his stuff already and he just wants me there for moral support. This news heartens me but is only a brief interlude and before long he's back onto Shirley being a slag and the landlord being a bastard again. Finally we get to the Infirmary and he has to shut up and give me directions because I can't remember where the place is.

There's a parking space right outside but it's a top flat. Having scaled the stairs and coughed up a few lung slugs, we ring for ages until a tired angry-looking bird in a dressing gown answers the door. She barely acknowledges us and skulks back to her room before we have time to say anything. Dave runs up to the next level to look for the landlord, discovers he hasn't arrived and so we sit in the kitchen next to the main door.

'What time did he say he'd be here?'

Dave stabs at the face of his watch.

'Now! Three minutes ago! It's a wind-up I bet. If I was late he'd charge me another day's rent. You honestly won't believe this guy.'

As I look around the kitchen it strikes me as unnaturally clean for a communal hovel. Even the floor is shining. Do people actually clean kitchen floors?

'Is this what E coli's done to folk? Kitchens aren't supposed to look like this, it's spotless.'

Dave looks amused.

'Aye, it has to be. The landlord's wife lets herself in all the time and if there's a dish on the bunker or a bean on the cooker she cleans it up and charges us all eight quid.'

'Naw!'

'Honestly, even if it's clean when she comes round she stands with a dishtowel in her hand till someone notices and pretends she had to clean it. I'm going to shop her to the Inland Revenue, ugly cow.'

'They can't do that, surely?'

'You better believe it. It's small print on the lease, funny wording you know. This is one of the better ones as well. You'll love them, I tell you. You'll want to sell up the two-bedroom bachelor pad in Jock's Lodge and move in.'

I laugh more than necessary, just to encourage him to keep lightened up about the whole thing. The Prozac seem to be making him paranoid, I've heard they can do that. Dave stares around the room like it's someone he hates and is about to smack in the face.

'How many people stay here, like? I thought it would be stowed-out with patchouli-oil-smelling-greasy-types making their beanfeasts and fish fingers.'

'Naw, there's just a couple of foreign students, you know the well-behaved kind. The rest are shift workers – bakers, a bus driver, cleaners, that sort of thing. They're usually in their beds by the time I get home. I've been here six months and still don't really know who actually lives here. I saw this

Arab guy coming out the bath the other day I didn't know from Adam, he could have come in off the street, I wouldn't be any the wiser. Still, it's a thousand times better than my mother's.'

I'm finding this all mildly educational in a morbid sort of way though I can't really see what he's moaning about – clean kitchen, cable TV, no noise, no hassle, nobody watching what you're doing. Then I hear a key in the door and this short-arse Barry McGuigan guy walks in with a Janis Joplin-type pig of a woman. The wee guy addresses Dave in an authoritative way and I realise he must be the landlord. He apologises for being late and seems OK but Dave has stiffened up and has a look of Linford Christie-like intensity about him. I follow them out the kitchen, up the staircase to Dave's bedroom where they make a big deal out of unlocking the door in our presence.

It's stark in there, like it's been burgled. We move what remains of Dave's stuff, which thankfully only amounts to his portable TV, video, Calor gas fire, duvet and bag of clothes because I'm getting pains in my chest after the first jaunt back up the stairs. The landlord and his wife stand just outside the door, don't help us but won't go in until we're ready. Two journeys is enough. We both stagger into the room, wheezing and coughing, and the odd couple follow us in and shut the door. I take an immediate dislike to them.

Barry McGuigan brings out a clipboard and Janis gets on the floor and starts snooping about. He begins studying the curtains as if they might hold a vital clue in a murder enquiry. She pulls the bed out and squints behind it.

'John, over here. There's some sellotape on the back of the headboard.'

Her man goes over and has a good look at it.

'No, it's OK. I think it's ours,' and they both go off

searching again and there's just this silence as they pad about taking themselves very seriously. Eventually Barry's standing frowning at a slight discoloration on the ancient wallpaper above the radiator and Janis is fingering a slight scratch on the wardrobe door.

'This is going to need decorated. It looks terrible. I've noticed you dry clothes on this radiator, Dave, that's what's caused it. I'm afraid we'll have to take something off the deposit to get it sorted out.'

'And this, John, look!' Janis says, staring at the wee line on the wood as if the room might collapse because of it.

Shorty gets all school-teacherly with Dave now.

'We have to charge for these things, Dave, I'm sorry. We don't want to rent out substandard accommodation to people and it shouldn't really be up to us to pay if someone damages our property, should it?'

Dave just raises his eyebrows. The woman is still stroking the dressing table, waiting to get her bit in. 'This will probably need French polishing, John, it's got quite a deep gash. What happened to it, Dave?'

'It's always been there, hasn't it? I've never even noticed it before.'

The landlord starts thumbing through the papers on his clipboard then points at some small print on one of the back pages.

'I don't think so, Dave, look this is the inventory you signed when you moved in. *Wooden double wardrobe with 12 hangers, quantity 1, remarks on condition, blank*. I think we might have noticed a dirty great scratch like that when we were making up the inventory, don't you? If it was there when you moved in why didn't you mention it when you checked the inventory?'

Officious little prick. In any other situation I'd have taken a swing at him but it's none of my business. I try to reason with him none the less.

'I'd hardly say it had any effect on the function of the wardrobe though, doesn't it say something in there about reasonable wear and tear?'

The pseudo-business persona drops slightly, and the hard wee bastard he probably once was before he started assaulting people financially rears up and begins shouting.

'Look at the state of it? Would you like it if I came round your house and ran a knife across your dining table, eh? It's a different story if it's someone else's property, eh?'

Dave looks very upset.

'Look, it doesn't matter, OK. Just tell me how much I'm getting back. I don't care if the bloody thing was scratched when I moved in or not.'

The landlord glares at me to keep out of it so he can railroad my weaker friend. He gets his silly wee clipboard out again and pulls off a sheet of paper with a long-looking sum on it.

'Here you are then, Dave. I think we've been more than fair, the kitchen we sent you all letters about, Jane had to clean it nineteen times but we've split that between the eight rooms so it's just £19 each.'

'Hey, half the time she was cleaning it to show people round to replace the folk you chucked out. You can't charge for that surely?'

Back to his justify-everything clipboard.

'Yes, section 6(a) on your lease says *tenants will ensure the property is in a clean and tidy condition for viewing by prospective tenants*,' then he turns to pig woman. 'He thinks we could have got someone to move in with the kitchen in that state.'

'If you didn't throw people out for nothing in the first place you wouldn't have to worry about it.'

'I wasn't talking to you, I was talking to my wife.'

I'm willing Dave to just take the money so we can get out of here. I get the impression the guy's trying to get one of us to hit him so he can screw a bit of criminal injuries compensation out of it all as well.

'Look, can you just get on with it? I have things to do, I have to find somewhere to live.'

He moves down to the next item on his list.

''Right, section 6(c), *the tenant undertakes to have the windows cleaned regularly.* I know for a fact you haven't touched these windows since you moved in. It looks like a doss house in here from the street.' Walking over to the window he runs his finger down the glass then shoves his stoorey digit in front of Dave's face. 'Do you really think it's up to Jane or me to clean your muck off the windows?'

'Next!'

'Subsection 6(c)ii, *the tenant shall ensure the fridge and freezer are defrosted on a weekly basis.* Do you want to take a look at them with us now? I'm sure you must have noticed the state they're in. We don't need to provide facilities like that but we try to keep a nice house here, make people comfortable. So unless you want to defrost them both now I'm going to have to take something off for that as well.'

I'm going to go out and wait in the car if he comes out with any more of this crap.

'So is that it then? How much are you giving me back?'

'Just a couple more things, Dave. First, you'll no doubt recall the hoover breaking a month or so ago and maybe also have noticed it was replaced within a week. Also, since you moved in we've had to replace the iron three times.'

'I have my own iron. I've never used any of yours.'

'They've all said that so far. Someone must have used it, you see my point? Why don't you show me your iron?'

'I moved it out at the weekend.'

The landlord tuts.

'I think £68 is a fair figure for all that. If you have a problem with anything I can go through the lease with you and explain it.'

Thankfully Dave submits.

'Forget it. Could I just have the money you owe me please?'

The landlord goes back over to the stain on the wallpaper.

'And then of course there's this. I'm going to have to get a decorator in for this. Jane and I don't have time to do it ourselves and I'll have to take something off to get something done to that dressing table, shall we say £190?'

'Aye right! You're kidding me?'

'It's all made perfectly clear here, Dave. We did ask you to read the lease carefully before you signed it. So £258 from £360, that's what, £102. Have you got the cheque book, Jane?'

Janis slithers over and hands him it.

'I'd have decorated the place myself if you'd asked me. You can't do that.'

'Look, do you want the money now or do you want to go crying to the Housing Department like that last pair? It didn't get them anywhere, did it?'

It's the most ridiculous legitimate robbery I've ever encountered in my life but I just want him to accept it. I just want out of there and a pint of Stella in my hand. Sod this bastard.

Dave watches him write the cheque then asks him to put his card number on the back.

'I'm afraid I don't carry them about together, you get warned against it. Especially in a place like this,' he sneers, holding up the cheque.

Dave swipes it from him then makes for the door and I hear him thundering down the stairs before I register that I'm left standing alone in the room with the pair of them. I look at the bastard and shake my head.

'You ought to be fucking ashamed.'

As I follow Dave down the stairs the shitehouse shouts after me, 'That's the price of being fucking wealthy I suppose.'

When I get down to the car Dave is leaning against the roof in tears. Jesus. I put my hand on his shoulder and he snorts and wipes his face and shakes his body together again.

'I forgot to get my cooking stuff, not that I can afford to find anywhere to cook now anyway.'

Encouraging him to get in the car I go round to the other door. When I get in he's sitting shaking his head.

'I'm sorry you had to listen to all that Darren. I wanted you to see what they were like though, I knew you didn't believe me.'

His perception freaks me out slightly and I don't really know what to say. I just want this part of the evening behind us and the drinking part to commence.

'You need to drown your sorrows, don't you think? There must be a way you can get back at the bastards. C'mon, we'll go down Lothian Road for a few beers and plot your revenge, eh?'

Dave agrees on the understanding he buys the drink to pay me back. He's got cash on him and isn't going to find anywhere to live for £102 so I don't allow myself to feel bad about it.

We drive round the corner to the car park at the top of Morrison Street. I know that if I get too pissed I can always get a taxi and pick the car up in the morning but I know I'll probably just drive home anyway. They never stop anyone midweek. Handing the emergency flask of malt I keep in the glove compartment to Dave I find myself actually starting to warm to him slightly. If I can just get him reminiscing about Aberdeen and off his problems. Knocking back a little anaesthetic he stares out into the night and exhales through a wide open mouth. I take a swig myself and watch the fumes turn into steam as I let out a little gasp of pleasure.

We go to the Burnt Post first. The Isle of Jura's a pound a nip and there's a quiz on which should be good for the awkward silences I'm anticipating. Nonetheless Dave still keeps going on about the landlord, and the other tenants not getting their deposits back and the good old days when the Bru would pay for a penthouse in Palmerston Place, so we end up missing half the questions. Also, the female quizmaster takes about ten minutes between each one to natter to her friends and at half-time we see her giving them some of the answers. But I persevere because Dave is buying me double malts and half pints of some lethal syrupy ale that gives me a buzz in the bollocks every time I take a slug.

By the time the second half of the quiz starts though, Dave is starting to get a bit verbal, banging his glass down on the table every time he's taken a drink as if he wants it to break, giving the evil eye to a teenager in a Rangers scarf doing the quiz with his dad. I convince him that we should go for a late drink at Dario's. He just needs a bit of fresh air, something to eat and he'll be OK. Besides, I really have my drinking head on now and I'm not nearly ready to go home.

As we cross Bread Street Dave waits on the island until a car comes, then walks out onto the road so it has to swerve to avoid him. As the driver skilfully manoeuvres to save his life Dave kicks the bumper and swears after him. I go back onto the road and pull him onto the pavement. Bloody arsehole. If he starts getting all destructive I'll just leave him. It was like this when we were at Aberdeen. Most of the time he was a timid, friendly sap of a guy but when he got on the Kestrel Superstrengths or spirits this nasty, sadistic character used to surface that would swear at old ladies, put broken glasses on the dance floor at nightclubs and pull the number plates off Porsches when we were walking home. I sort of hoped he'd grown out of all that.

Dario's is virtually empty, which I'm glad about as the less people to possibly antagonise Dave the better. I'm past eating and just want to carry on throwing booze down my neck but order a margherita to justify my being there. Dave just wants chips, which is a bit embarrassing, but the waiter obliges nonetheless since the place isn't exactly heaving. We drink bottled lager as the draught stuff in these places is generally pish and they charge you over the odds for sixth of a gill measures.

Dave gulps down half his beer in one then gets his elbows on the table and looks me in the eye in a worrying way.

'I've got an idea. An indirect way of getting the rest of the deposit back.'

Oh, here we go again.

'Honest, Dave, you should put it behind you. There's nothing you can do about it, just try and blank it.'

'Won't you just listen to my idea? It's a cracker, honestly.'

I submit.

'OK, right, we have a few pints then we drive back round there, I got an extra set of keys cut. They'll all have been in their beds for hours. Know that shiny new microwave that was in the kitchen?'

I know exactly what he means.

'You can't steal the microwave. He'll know who it was right away.'

'Aye but he doesn't know where I've moved to. As far as he knows I'm on the streets. C'mon, there's a decent video in there as well. Honestly it'll be the easiest thing you've ever done.'

'No way, Dave. You're pissed, it's seriously not a good idea.' I start suggesting other methods of revenge. 'Where does he live? Someone told me if you superglue coins to locks you can't separate them, you have to take the door off. Do it to his house. Do it to his car, no?'

It's like he doesn't even hear me.

'Listen, they'll all be asleep, really. We just let ourselves in, pick the stuff up and leave. Nobody's going to see us. They're used to hearing people rustling about in the middle of the night. Nothing could be simpler.'

The waiter brings over our food and Dave orders another two bottles of Becks and a couple of doubles.

'Come on, pal, it'll be just like uni. Remember the time we stole that Iraqi guy's bed? Or that raincoat with the big holes in the pockets you used to go into Waterstone's with. Selling course books to everyone at a fiver a piece.'

I'm pissed off he's mentioned that and worried about what he might bring up next. The anticipation of it is almost enough to agree.

'Come on, Dave, that was nearly fifteen years ago. It's a

little bit different when you've got a mortgage and a job and all that sort of shit to consider.'

'Aye, one of us does.'

Bastard. I hate being put in corners like this.

'You'll get on your feet again. You've still got your job.'

'By my tooth-skin.'

I start asking him about work to take his mind off cat-burglary but he won't allow me to sidetrack him.

'Sod all that. I don't give a damn about it any more. At the moment all that matters to me is getting even with that bastard.'

'It's just so sort-of scummy. Stealing. It's not the right way to get back at him, it just makes you as bad as them.'

'Oh come on, since when did you get so self-righteous about stealing? I seem to recall the Darren Unauthorised Investment Trust not so long ago. I'm talking a microwave and video, something you probably wouldn't even get a custodial sentence for. You'd do at least five years if they found out about that.'

I try to get him to lower his voice. Since he found out about all that a couple of years ago I've just sort of been hoping he'd miraculously forgotten about it. Not that he'd ever tell anyone, which is probably the reason I told him in the first place, but you can't take risks with things like that. Dave's plan does seem trivial in comparison though. Maybe it'll even things up between us.

'You're right, Dave, my heid's up my arse. Some of the things we did at uni though, that thing with the shite in the computer room, remember, and the time you smashed all those windows?' We giggle into our beers in reflection. 'I better not get done for drunk driving though and they find the stuff in the car.'

'It'll be fine, we can go back to my place by the wee back streets, there's never any police along them. It's foolproof, I guarantee.'

We both have another nip and a Becks to steady ourselves. I pick some of the topping off my pizza as Dave holds up a soggy french fry and begins a tirade about the joys of home-made chips. The fact that he is starting to perk up and even occasionally laugh and smile justifies what we're about to do in my mind. The truth is, though, I'm actually starting to feel a bit excited about the whole thing. Then I make the mistake of asking him what went wrong between him and Shirley and he gets on a bit of a downer again so we have to have another couple of drinks till he calms down.

We're both slaughtered by the time we leave so I ask the guy if I can have the rest of my pizza in a doggy bag and we start hassling them to sell us a half bottle of Grouse. At first they say they don't have any to take away but we go on at them so much they pour 35cl into a coke bottle for us. I'm not aware that either of us seem particularly aggressive, just radge sort of drunk, but they seem really nervous and submissive.

Neither of us are staggering but we agree to cross back over to the car park in silence so we don't draw attention to ourselves. We walk past the kebab shop then round the back of the ABC so no one will clock us walking straight from the pub to the car. The streets are deserted, hardly any traffic, so we get there and round to Tollcross with the minimum difficulty. Although we remain silent once we're in the safe cocoon of the car I can feel the excitement buzzing between us.

We park just round the corner from the flat. The street is deserted. It's sheltered housing opposite and down at the bottom of the street so hopefully no one will be passing by at this time of night. Both taking a slug for stealth from the cola bottle, I lock the car and we walk round. The climb up the stairs to the door of the flat subdues the excited feeling I'm having but I'm still getting a sort of high from it all.

The main hall is in darkness apart from a strip of light above the fuse box. We leave it like that then put the door on the snib and feel our way up to the living room door. The house is in silence apart from the fridge buzzing through in the kitchen. Dave feels around for the lamp switch and we liberate the video from the spaghetti of wires behind the telly. He tells me to take it down and wait for him and switches the kitchen light on as he holds the door open for me.

I'm laughing to myself as I carry it downstairs on tiptoes. I've got this great buzz of achievement, a real sort of hit you only get when you're doing something illegal. I'd forgotten the amazing adrenaline rush you get from stealing, a sort of trembly euphoric feeling not a hundred miles away from an orgasm. I manoeuvre the stair door open with the slight mobility I have in my pinkie and foot then I'm off down the street and away round the corner, and nobody's there, nobody's looking, it's a fucking cinch. I beep the doors open with my keyring as I approach the car, putting the video down briefly while I open the boot. I feel like a master criminal. I feel great.

Leaving the boot unlocked I get in the car, light a fag and suck the top of the coke bottle. The adrenaline is firing through me. Turning the ignition I put the radio on and it's that There's No Limit-thing which just seems to add to my feeling of power. *No limit we'll reach for the sky, no valley too deep, no mountain too high* . . . and I'm jigging about in my seat, slugging back the Grouse and feeling like a king.

Then the song finishes and the three o'clock news comes on. Nothing exciting though, no gruesome murders or terrible rapes, no drunk drivers in Lothian Road or video thefts in Tollcross. I'm just wanting another record to come on. Something to sustain this great fucking feeling. Next up's some darky female singing a love song though, which is not what I'm after. I start twiddling about with the stations, trying to find something appropriate, then hear a wee snippet of conversation that I think might be interesting and listen till it bores me so I swivel on from station to station again. Then I listen to a little bit of a record I like, then some guy talking about what a sad man Tommy Burns must be and then I start to become conscious of the fact that time has passed. I've been sitting here a wee while now and Dave is still not down with the microwave. It's 3.07 on the clock and I remember listening to the three o'clock news and a record before that and my mind begins playing with all sorts of possibilities. I look up the street but it's still dead. What the fuck is going on?

What if he's been caught? What if one of the flatmates that does know him has got up for a dump and caught him tiptoeing out the flat with the microwave? What would they do? Would they phone the landlord? He could be on his way round here now. I try to think of some reasonable explanation as to how it could possibly take him fifteen minutes to unplug an oven and carry it down three flights of stairs. I take another slug of the whisky and light another fag and toy with the idea of just leaving him, then wonder if I should go somewhere and dump the video in case the police turn up in the morning. Fucking hell, I don't need this. I'm just starting to look out the window for somewhere I could put the video so it might look like a burglar's lost his nerve when I see a movement in the mirror out the corner of my eye and Dave's coming towards me with the microwave. Thank fuck.

As I get out to open the boot for him I sense that everything's all right, that there's not a flatmate behind him in his jammies. When we get back in the car I realise he's fucking beaming, huge grin on his face, giggling.

'Where the fuck did you get to? Did someone see you?'

Dave reaches for the bottle and gestures me to calm down.

'No problem, pal, it's all right. I was just making some proper chips,' and he lifts up his hands as if in explanation. I look at them for enlightenment but they just look normal, dirty nails the bastard has though.

'What are you on about? You've been about twenty minutes. I was about to bury the video in the Meadows.'

He continues smiling away to himself, trying to calm me down, laughing away about his chips until I begin to accept that it must be OK. Dave seems in no hurry to go anywhere so I take his word that no one's caught him.

'It was good though, eh? An amazing hit you get doing stuff like that.'

The radio's playing another dance record I don't recognise now and I start thinking about how good I felt when I first got back to the car.

'Can we go round to the Meadows for a wee while? Take the pizza and the whisky. Have a wee celebratory picnic?'

I'm sort of game because I don't really want to go home while I'm still buzzing and despite all I've drunk the thieving has given me second wind.

We drive round and park in Roseneath Terrace then walk down to the top of the Meadows with the coke bottle of whisky and the pizza. It's a clear night and despite the haze of the street lights you can see the stars clearly. Whole little galaxies in which even smaller galaxies appear if you stare long enough. We wolf down the pizza, our appetites enlivened by the high we both feel. Ecstasy probably feels like this. Why pay £15 for a dodgy aspirin though when you can just go and chorey some electrical goods? I feel absolutely fearless now we're away from it all. Even if the landlord goes round in the morning and thinks it was Dave then that's his problem. I went to get the deposit back with him but nobody's actually seen us together since we left the restaurant. If the worst comes to the worst I can say I got a taxi outside Dario's. The riskiest part is over.

We used to lie on the beach at Aberdeen and look at the stars like this. Argue about which one was which. Dave must be thinking the same thing because he slugs at the bottle then points up at the big bright one in the middle, the one I've been staring at.

'Go on then, what one's that?'

'Too easy.'

'Go on then, Patrick Moore, tell me.'

'It's the fucking North Star, isn't it?'

'No chance, if that's the North Star what's that doing over there?'

And then we start, arguing over the stars, fighting about the universe, like we're gods arguing over territory. I feel really quite fond of the guy. It's like we're on something. We sit there for about half an hour, gabbing on to each other, necking back the booze until the bottle is empty and, naked without the alcohol to sustain the closeness we've just had, quieten down again.

As we begin walking back to the car I think over what we've done. The high I feel now seems more related to the stars. I'm conscious of being terrestrial again as the long grassy plains of the Meadows drop back down into focus and the sound of sirens punctuates our universe. Dave stops and looks back over in the direction of the flats. The siren noises are getting louder and louder. I stand waiting for him, wondering what the fuck he's looking at. I hope he isn't getting maudlin again. He'll be home in ten minutes, he can be miserable then. The siren sound is echoing round the whole of the Meadows. You can't get a sense of what direction it's coming from. Then it stops.

'Do you think we're about to be pulled by the fuzz?' I laugh, trying to establish contact with him again.

Dave doesn't even smile.

'Nah, it's fire engines. Someone's gone home drunk and left the chip pan on, nothing surer. It happens all the time.'

The Hard Sell

HE WAS JUST some man from her evening class. The one who distracted every lesson by bleating on, questioning every basic point, making the lecturer squirm amid his tirades of misapprehension and innuendo. She remembered a paper on D H Lawrence that he'd addressed the group with, po-faced and indignant as the rest of the class tried, unsuccessfully, to stifle laughter. How he'd blethered on about 'prick envy' and emphatically espoused that Lawrence based Lady Chatterley's lover's occupation on the fact that 'she was game and he wanted to keep her'.

She found him vaguely amusing in an irritating sort of way and was pleased that he was so thoroughly infatuated with himself and the sound of his own pseudo-Transatlantic Castlemilk drone. This reduced the likelihood of her having to speak in class. Not that she didn't have things to say, but, unlike him, she was sheepish about airing her working-class voice amid this otherwise middle-class audience.

When the bell rang at nine o'clock, signalling the end of the final lesson, she slammed her book shut victoriously. Two hours a week for twenty-eight weeks and she'd succeeded in never uttering a word. Liberated by this accomplishment she agreed to go for a farewell tipple with a few people from the class.

As she stood by the bar awaiting her drink she glanced

across at the group as they argued over seating arrangements and noticed the bletherer staring straight across. Looking him in the eye, she expected him to divert his glance but he continued glaring at her. Several uncomfortable seconds passed before he smiled, looked away and she saw him beckon for a pint at the far side of the bar. Returning to her senses as the barman shoved her drink in front of her, she fumblingly paid. She stood nervously clinking the ice in her glass, too agitated to look over again, ashamed with herself for wanting to. Taking a long drink she felt the whisky and coke burn its way down, calming her.

'Are you finally gonna speak tonight then, Lizzie?'

As he offered his hand to shake, she let out a slight squeal. He squeezed her fingers until she was forced into eye contact with him then he gestured to an empty table by the window.

'I hope you dinnae think I'm being a bit forward, like, but I've been trying to work up the nerve to speak to you for weeks. I guess tonight's my last chance.'

Was this a compliment of sorts? Could she even remember what a compliment sounded like?

'I guess it is.'

Putting on his best bashful face he continued.

'Please don't think I'm a weirdo. I don't want to invade your space or anything. It's just, I dunno, like I feel really drawn to you. You know, I find you attractive but it's more than that, sort of. You know? Am I making any sense or are you looking for the nearest exit?'

Ushering her into a window seat separate from the main group, he squeezed in beside her.

And then he began to talk. And talk and talk and talk. If he hadn't heard her voice before he certainly wasn't remedying that now. He told her about his Lawrence essay, regaling her with his theories on 'prick envy', waxing lyrical about Freud as if Freud were a character in a Carry On film. Then she got the life and times of his mother – how emancipated she was, how she was born too soon, how she singlehandedly brought about the sexual revolution in the South Side of Glasgow. But most of all he talked about his job. He was a salesman and, in his own opinion, was one of the best. Although he'd sold everything in his time – houses, cars, slave labour, ladies underwear, LSD, insurance – he'd lost his nerve to go it alone a couple of years into the recession and was now manager of an electrical goods store run by one of the large chains. Commission-only was too risky nowadays, apparently. There was a time when he could clear a thousand a week but now he was struggling to feed his kids. Gone were the holidays in Florida, gone were his Hugo Boss suits and gone was his prized Jaguar. He told her his golden rules of selling – unnerve them with eye contact, find out their first name and use it, then touch them. Make the customer feel like your lover and don't bother with Asians as they like to listen to you talk for hours but never buy anything.

He insisted on buying all the drinks, and she, not used to being out on her own and therefore short of cash, submitted. As soon as her glass was two-thirds empty he'd be up at the bar for another double. As she became loosened by the drink she felt bold enough to occasionally meet his constant gaze.

'These rules don't just apply to selling though. It's all about manipulation through body language. I'm gonna write a book about it wunna these days . . .'

He moved a few strands of hair from her eyes.

'It's all about being able to spot a good lead and not giving up till you get what you want.'

She smiled as he took her hand.

'And what is a good lead?'

He kissed her cheek and looked at her earnestly.

'I'm sort of hoping you are. I don't know if you're gonna let me close the deal though.'

He squeezed her fingers.

'Come on, Lizzie. I know how to really please a woman. You know what they say – fishing for the good times starts with throwing in your line.'

She looked slightly puzzled.

'Who said that?'

'I did but Tom Waits ripped me off,' he laughed but she didn't get the joke.

He put his arm around her, gave her a squeeze and kissed her ear.

'Oh, Lizzie, Lizzie, Lizzie. You realise you have the power to make an extremely well-endowed salesman very happy.'

She raised her eyebrows.

'Awe, c'mon Lizzie, let's fart in the face of piety.'

As he kissed her neck and her little silver crucifix, she reluctantly felt her neglected libido slowly flicker into motion. She was responding. Go go go. He brushed his knuckle absentmindedly against her breast.

'You're an incredible-looking woman, Lizzie, really unusual-looking. How old are you, if it's not awfie rude of me? Thirty-three? Thirty-four?'

'I was forty-four last month,' she beamed.

He looked astonished.

'You're having me on. You make me feel like John Hurt. I remember the first time I saw you at the class, you had on a red jacket and your hair was up, I thought, she is special, she is really something very special.'

As he stroked her hair he began nibbling at her earlobe. 'I like it better like this though, really womanly. Let's go somewhere else, Lizzie, please?'

And then, unable to think of another pleasant word to say to the woman, he grabbed her. They sat locked in a feverish tongue wrestle for the next ten minutes until she noticed over his shoulder the group they had originally come in with, staring at them open-mouthed.

Gently pushing him off, she gestured to the group, who all self-consciously looked away. He got the message nonetheless, lifted her coat from the chair, stood up and helped her into it. Never underestimate the power of nosy bastards, he thought as he led her out of the pub.

As soon as they were on the other side of the door they both burst into fits of giggles and cuddled each other.

'Did they see us, Lizzie? I completely forgot they were there.'

She held on to the collar of his coat, quite breathless from the laughing. He was tired of talking and pulled her into the grounds of the bowling club next door. They walked past the main club house towards the line of trees bordering the green itself, and he pinned her against the wall.

Hastily unfastening her blouse, he chewed feverishly at her cleavage in a way that gave her a wonderful shuddery sensation. Breaking away from her he stepped back to unzip his trousers and ordered her to take off her knickers. She slid off her tights as seductively as possible and asked him if he should perhaps use a condom.

'You're a bit old for babies, aren't you?' he chuckled, guiding himself into her.

She hadn't noticed how big he was but she could feel a pain in her stomach each time he shoved in. She'd never felt that with her husband but then again he was hung like a child and was a die-hard missionary man. The unfamiliar feeling of being stretched inside was thrilling although he kept slipping out as she was slightly taller than him.

'Turn around!' he ordered, moving her round to face the wall. This position was perfect for him but as he grunted against her, her hands and face scraped on the stone wall. She pulled away then kissed him and pulled him down to the ground. They lay half on the grass and half in a flower bed. He began jabbing her again, mumbling in her ear,

'Aye, you come out to do a nice little night class and end up with a length inside you . . . and you love it, don't you, you dirty, dirty woman?'

His hips moved faster and she kissed him and caressed his head in lewd delirium. Finally he shuddered to a halt and rolled onto his back with a clump of turf in his hand. She smiled into the darkness as they lay together in the wheezy silence then he grasped for her hand.

'Did I make you come?'

She smiled at him as if he were joking.

'No, no, I don't need to. I never have so I don't know what I'm missing.'

He looked disgruntled, let go of her hand, stood up and began dressing.

'Was I better than your old man then?'

She looked up in disbelief. 'That's a horrible question to ask. I'm not going to answer that.'

She suddenly noticed streaks of earth on his face where she had been pawing him but was too nervous to mention this as her reply seemed to have driven him into a profound sulk.

He finished dressing and looked at her in annoyance.

'Are you ready? I really have to make a move.'

Picking up her handbag she followed him out onto the street. There was a shitty silence as they walked back towards the pub. A taxi purred towards them and he stepped out between two parked cars and stopped it. He said a few words to the driver then shouted to her.

She walked towards him and entered the taxi, half-expecting him to get in, but he slammed the door behind her, wished her farewell and told the driver to take her where she wanted to go. She asked to be dropped at the bus stop around the corner as she didn't have much money and noticed that he didn't wave goodbye as she was driven at breakneck speed (the driver apparently trying to make a point), to the bus stop 200 yards away.

By the time the bus turned up about twenty minutes later she was starting to nip between the legs. Limping upstairs, she rifled her bag for her pocket mirror and as she shakily dabbed powder on her grazed forehead, the warm, meaty smell of their sex wafted up to her nostrils and made her wince.

Routes

IT'S MY TWELFTH birthday today. The poster at the bus stop has a photo of a sick-looking wee laddie and the words 'Getting Hold of Drugs isn't Difficult – Ask a 12-year-old'. If anyone asks me though I'm saying nothing or Scott will batter the shite out of me. Mum keeps her gear in a film spool holder on top of the unit in the living room in the fruit bowl with the plasters in it so I could take that any time I wanted but I dinnae. Drugs are shite. Scott gave me some draw once when he was pissed and I had a right whitey. It was like *The Evil Dead*, man. The wallpaper was coming all out at me and I puked up and I thought someone was pouring petrol through the letter box. Fucking horrible like. It doesnae do anything like that to mum or Scott though, they just lie vegging in front of the telly like they're sleeping or something. They might as well be, like, 'cause they dinnae talk or nowt. The only time they ever go out is when there's a tarry shortage. Then they go to the pub. It's like living with two bean bags except bean bags would be more fun 'cause at least you could jump about on them and slash them open and that. About once a year mum will speak, usually to get on her high horse and accuse Scott of shagging other women, as if that hackit puss could get anyone except her. Apart from that though there isnae much talking roond oor hoose.

Maybe Scott will do a runner when mum has the baby.

They dinnae even have enough money for me so I dinnae ken why she's having another one. Maybe they'll see what this one's like then get rid of me, not that I'd care. Aren't folk supposed to stop smoking when they're going to have a baby anyway? All the fumes she sooks in'll probably choke the poor wee bastard. It'll probably be born dead, if it's lucky.

When I left tonight the radiators were on full because the electric meter had turned back too much so mum was slobbing around in just her leggings with her gigantic belly and her disgusting sticky-out belly button like something out of *Alien*. Her tits are fucking disgusting with all blue bits sticking out of them like that posh foreign cheese you get with the germs in it. It'll probably put me off women for life, not that I was ever on them to begin with. You shouldnae walk about like that in front of your bairn though. Why can they no just pay the proper bill like everybody else?

I asked them for a pair of Nike Air trainers for my birthday. Instead I got this bogging pair of fucking plimsolls with pink bits and a wee tongue, like fucking lassies' ones. Mum probably got them in Asda. I'll never wear them. I'd get my head kicked in if I wore them. Then she gives me these fucking horrible school clothes, like blue shirts and shite that she's supposed to get with my child benefit anyway, but she gives me them today and says they're like birthday presents? Aye right. I ken we're no exactly loaded but even wee ten-year-old schemies fae Broomhouse have got Reeboks these days, you know, they still manage no to dress like complete neds.

If they didnae spend all their money on vodka and blow and fags they couldae got me something decent. Scott gave me a fiver in a card with a fucking bunny rabbit on the front. Fucking generous, eh? Some of my pals get a tenner pocket money every fucking week of the year. That cunt stays with us for nothing and gets all his food and blow and bevvy so he's got his whole giro to himself. Tight bastard.

They could've even had a wee party for me or something, d'you no think? I'm sure they could have got someone to come. Folk'll go to parties even if they hate the cunt whose birthday it is. But what did they do instead? Mum bought a Mr Kipling's exceedingly shitey cake and didn't even put a candle on it, no expense spared, ken? When I went to have a second bit, Scott said, 'D'you want a nose-bag with that, you greedy wee bastard?'

That's why I've come out, that and I can't stand the sub-fucking-tropical temperature and auld cheesy tits snoring on the settee. Fuck the pair of them, I hate both their guts. All they care about is themselves, they dinnae even like me. She's my mum and she doesnae even like me. It makes me feel barrie, you know?

I'm gonnae stay out late so they think something bad's happened to me. If they think I'm dead they might realise they'd miss me. Maybe it'll make them nice to me for a wee while. So that's it, I'm staying out till they think someone's murdered me.

The bus is taking ages to come. It doesnae matter what time you go for a bus it's always at least twenty minutes before it's due. I get whatever one comes first but it always seems to be a 2 or a 6. The 6 is perfect because it misses out Princes Street, goes down to the docks and the seaside and then it turns at the terminus and comes right back so you dinnae have to get off and stand about somewhere funny. Buses always finish up in these slightly scary places but that's sort of why I like getting on them in the first place. Buses are the best! I dinnae ken why folk stand in shop doorways or waste money going to the pictures and that when they could just cruise about on buses. If you've got a bus pass like me it doesnae cost nowt.

Mind you, standing about waiting on them really shites me off. There's always either none at all or big convoys of the fuckers. They probably have to go round in big groups 'cause the drivers are such arses some cunt would kill one of them if they were on their own.

It's fucking bitter standing here. My jeans are so cold it feels like I've pissed myself. I dinnae have a jacket on because I've only got my blazer and it's bad enough wearing that cunting thing to school. When I grow up I'm going to design my own computer games, really brilliant, impossible ones. Much better than any of that shite on *Gamesmaster*. I'll be fucking raking it in and I won't give mum or Scott a penny, in fact I probably won't even have to talk to them any more so they can just piss off. I have to get really rich. It's the only way I'll get away from them, unless they just chuck me out anyway then I'll probably end up having to go with old perverts just to buy food. Aye, being twelve is fucking brilliant so far.

Several days later a 44 comes. I've never got on a 44 before, it says it goes to Wallyford – sounds like the sort of place Scott might come from. I ask the driver if he goes back to Longstone after Wallyford. He does so I get on then the cunt calls me back and says I can't get on 'cause it'll take about three hours. I tell him I dinnae mind, I just want to get on then he swears for no reason and all the passengers start nebbing like, trying to see what the hold-up is. Rotten bastard! What harm am I doing? It's no like I'm out choreying cars or spray-painting Paki shops. How is it no matter what I do it's always wrong?

Folk dinnae like things they don't understand. Folk cannae understand me.

Normally I sit next to the driver in case there's trouble but I go upstairs tonight because I've got a beamer about all the shite he gave me. You always get all the weirdos upstairs. Last time I sat up here this drunk guy did a piss up the back and it was like running up and down the bus every time it stopped, fucking bogging, man. It's best to sit up the back so you can see all that's going on, although it's just some old dear and a Chinkie guy so it's OK the now. Chinkies make me feel sort of like, safe. I dinnae really ken why though 'cause they're in these Triad gangs and that, but they just do it to each other, see, and then they get all their violence out that way so they dinnae need to do it to other folk. I wish I was a Chinkie. They're all Ninjas and no other cunt understands what they say or their writing and that, it's so fucking cool.

I'm going to have my sweets now in case it gets busy. I got a Mars bar, crisps and a Twix with some of Scott's money. The Paki didnae have any Monster Munch so I had to get like normal shitey ones – fucking salt and vinegar as well, I dinnae even really like them. You crunch each crisp down though and store it in your cheek, then when you've got them all there you sook and sook all the flavour out then eat the soggy bit. It's brilliant. The only way to eat crisps, man. The vinegar makes my mouth go all in though. I should have got some Red Card.

Next I have the Mars bar to try and get some spit back into my mouth. I bite the chocolate off the sides, then gnaw the nougat bit and scrape the toffee off the top bit with my bottom teeth. Then I sook all the rest of the toffee off the bit chocolate and let it lie on my tongue till it melts. It's hard to just keep it there without eating it, but. These fucking cooking programmes mum watches all day go on about how to make stuff and that but they dinnae have any about how to eat it. I'd go on that. I ken how to eat stuff best, how to eat each bit of a bar of chocolate separately. It's a gift like.

Last of all I have the Twix 'cause I always leave the best one till the end. With the Twix you bite the chocolate off the sides like with the Mars bar then once you get the rest of the chocolate off the biscuit bit (you cannae break it, mind) you can do two things. Either bite the toffee off and then sook the bit biscuit or eat the biscuit, roll the toffee bit in your hand and then eat it like a big toffee ball. That's the best way but I sometimes eat the biscuit last if I'm in the right mood.

A guy comes upstairs with a wee girl as I wipe my chocolatey hands on my jeans. Just finished in time. The wee girl kneels up on the seat and looks back at the rest of us. I hate when that happens and some lippy wee sprog starts slagging you and you cannae say anything back. No this one though, she starts giggling, squirming around on the seat, saying, 'Nigger, daddy. Nigger, nigger.'

Her dad smiles and looks all embarrassed.

'Stop that, that's not a nice thing to say.'

That just makes her worse though.

'Nigger, daddy, funny nigger, eh, what's that daddy, nigger . . . nigger . . .'

The dad just points out the window, trying to take her mind off it.

'Look, see the big clock. What time is it? Tell daddy what time it is.'

'Nigger, see it, daddy, nigger.'

You can tell the other people on the bus are listening but they're pretending not to. Some are having a sly wee smile to themselves. The Chinkie guy's looking out the window but you can tell he's all tensed up and that. The wee girl seems to know she's got an audience so she's away again.

'Daddy, daddy, I spy nigger. Can we do I spy nigger?'

Her dad's fucking beaming now. He doesnae ken what to do, really cringing like. The wee lassie just keeps going on and on until the bus gets to the next stop, he freaks, picks her up round the waist and carries her off screaming. From the window I watch him pointing at her, really angry like, then up at the bus but she's just laughing, thinking it's a big joke. When the bus eventually pulls away the Chinkie guy clears his throat and looks down at his legs, embarrassed like. Poor cunt, she probably didnae even mean him, she didnae ken. It wasnae like she meant any harm. She probably heard it in one ay they Ice Cube films or a Public Enemy record. You dinnae even hear white folk saying it these days, it's no allowed.

These black rapper films are fucking magic, though. The kids all carry AK47s and call everyone muthafucka and talk in that fucking brilliant sort of jive rap that white cunts cannae understand. I wish I was a fucking young blood in the Bronx or something, they have the coolest fucking clothes of anyone – no fucking blazers and Asda trainers but they're fucking poorer than any cunt. White people are just so fucking boring like, they don't do nothing muthafucka!

Even Pakis are better than whites. Like this Paki in our street got married the other week and they had like balloons and fucking fairy lights and streamers and stuff all over the front of the house and in the garden and that, and on the day the guy got married he came doon the street on a white horse. No kidding, with his fucking turban on and everything. I was pissing myself, it was like Channel 4 on a Sunday afternoon. Much cooler than standing in a boring fucking church then getting forced to do the dashing shite sergeant with your narky wee cousin. I dinnae like that Paki dancing they make us do at PE though. It's supposed to be just for lassies but we all have to do it 'cause they think it'll make us get on better with the Paki kids. I get on with them fine apart from that maya maya maya maya shite the Mr Woman we get for gym makes us do. It's all right for the lassies. They just say they've got their periods so it ends up with just the laddies doing fucking girly Paki dancing. I wish I had periods. I'd have them every fucking Wednesday.

A guy gets on and sits at the back with a bag of chips. They smell fucking beautiful, it's making me dribble. Folk shouldnae be allowed to eat stuff that smells like that in public unless they're willing to share them aboot a bit, don't you think? He's eating them really noisy though and you can hear the slavers all clicking about his mouth. It's fucking revolting, man.

This place we're at now is in the papers aw the time. It's where all the old poofy guys come to get off with young laddies like me, manky bastards. The laddies get loads of money for it though, it said. Some eleven-year-olds make £100 a night. I bet they've got Nike Air trainers. I always have a good look when the bus goes past but you never see nowt. I dinnae ken if it happens in they posh flats or they hang about the bushes next to that hill bit or what. Nothing's going on tonight though, just some awfie tall woman walking her dug. It's sort of exciting though, knowing bad stuff like that's going on but I'm up here safe on the bus. That young guy at the bus stop looks a bit poofy. Maybe he's just been doing it. If he gets on I can check the seat if he farts. Naw, he's not getting on, he's just hanging around waiting to pick up an old guy – dirty cunt.

It's dark now but the sky's still red round the buildings and the floodlights at Easter Road look like alien paratroopers just watching what's going on. There's no a match on the night though, it must just be training. Roy used to take me to Easter Road. Why did mum no just stick with him? It was good as well because he only ever came round during the day so mum would like play cards and Scrabble and that with me at night, or do my homework. Imagine her doing that now? She wouldnae be able to see the fucking book. Roy was like a real dad too. He didnae mind me being there like now, I think he even maybe liked me a wee bit. I used to get sweets from him when he came round and he'd even take us to the pictures and stuff. Mum doesn't even speak to him now though. When they first split up I thought he might still come round and see me 'cause we got on quite well and that but I huvnae see him since.

It wasn't like he was my proper dad though. I'm only allowed to mention him if I call him *that bastard*. I've never met him because mum really hates him and says I'm better not knowing about him. I'd really like to meet him, though, to see what he's like, you know, if he's like me at all. You'd think he'd be like me a bit like 'cause supposedly everything about people comes from their mums and dads and I'm fuck-all like mum, thank fuck, so most of my bits must come from dad. When I'm sixteen I'll find him and go and live with him. Mum probably makes all that stuff up about him just so I don't, just so she keeps getting the child benefit to buy her tarry with. One day I'm going to just get on a bus and never go back. They probably wouldn't even notice until they needed me to go to the chippie for munchies.

This bit now's where all the rich cunts stay. Big flash hooses with gardens the size of three back-greens and ponds and swings and tree-hooses and stuff. There's probably enough toys and computer games in each of them to do a whole school but they'll be too snobby to let any other cunt play with them. What a fucking waste. Who decides who gets rich mums and dads and who gets stuck with sorry poor fucks like mine? What did I do in an earlier life to deserve that pair? How could she no have had me adopted by some rich family with a tree-house and a CD-ROM who bought me Nike Air trainers and a Timberland jacket and a decent bike instead of that choreyed old wreck I have to go about on.

The unbelievable thing is mum actually thinks she's bringing me up well like. A plate of some horse's baws oot of Kwik-Save once a day and that fanny pretending to be my dad and I'm supposed to be fucking grateful or something? Like she made me watch this documentary about one of these social services homes for bad boys, you know, and said if I didnae behave she'd send me away to one. Fucking mental like, these places are brilliant. They've got snooker tables and swimming pools and everyone gets their own Sega and you live in a big room with all your pals and just muck about all the time. I started shoplifting after I saw that programme. Why won't that fucking Paki catch me? One time after I nicked a Snickers he put a sign on the door that said only two school children at a time so he must have seen. He must know.

I suppose if Scott left mum he'd take his Sega. Like the next guy she picks up might be nicer to me but there's no guarantee he'd have one too. Fuck, why is life so complicated? He's only got four games though – Prince of Persia which I cannae even work 'cause cunty-baws lost the wee book, some shitey Mickey Moose thing I dinnae play because the silly wee tune gets on my tits and Sonic 1 and 2 which were barrie for the first few months but once you get to the end it's shite. You can still go through it and try and get all the chaos emeralds and millions of rings and extra men but if you've already killed the evil doctor at the end there's no much point. Having to play it on the black and white telly in mum's bedroom makes it doubly shite but I only get near the colour one when they're in the pub. It's their fucking life source, see. I suppose I could chorey a few games and take them with me to the social services home when I got caught.

I'll maybe suffer them a wee bit longer though 'cause Scott's supposed to be getting a computer, like with a Pentium processor and that. These ones have got the Internet. That's a fucking amazing thing that. There's like porno films and every game ever invented and you can speak to folk anywhere in the world but they dinnae need to ken what you look like. You could get a photo of like one of Boyzone and pretend to some Paki burd in Jamaica that it's you.

This weird woman's sitting across from me now. I thought she was singing along to her Walkman but she's no, it's like gibberish oot the bible she's coming out with, real fucking strange stuff. Then I have a wee look and if the cunt's no sitting wi a fucking bible on her lap. What a radge. She's maybe in one ae they cults or a satanist or something. Completely mental like, coming out with really funny shit. And yeah he said he would smite them down, oh yes, he'll smite you down all right, sort yourselves out or he will smite you down! Fucking hell. Then she does a bit of the old What-a-Friend-We-Have-in-Jesus shite. It sort of looks like she's talking to the guy in front of her but she isnae. She's just sitting babbling away to herself, really twitchy like. This is giving me the serious shits. I really dinnae like fucking scary mental folk like this. I'm going downstairs in case she has an eppy and pulls out a kitchen knife and also so's I can have a wee neb on the way downstairs. Aaaaagh, fuck. The crazy bitch saw me looking at her and gave me a really scary look and says You look after your salvation, I'll look after mine. My legs go all shaky and I manage to crash into a seat downstairs before I fall over. Coorying against the window I have to huddle up to stop myself shaking. Talk aboot fucking psychos? I think the world's being taken over by mental cunts, they're everywhere nowadays. How's no one else noticed?

I try to concentrate on the tower blocks across in Kirkcaldy where my cousin Mark lives to take my mind off the spooky woman. You have to look really hard when it's dark but you can just make out some of the high-up windaes if you screw your eyes up. I'm squinting oot at this when the bus stops and standing in the queue is this fucking deformed guy. His mooth looks like someone's put a bit thread round his lips and pulled and one of his eyes is all sunken into his head like a fucking monster. His heid's fucking huge, man. Fucking hell, what's goin on here. I've never been past Eastfield before, I dinnae like this place. I have to go and sit beside the horrible driver because I'm really starting to shite it. Why did I no just go for the 6?

Wait a minute, there's Luca's ice-cream shop. I ken that place. Auntie Carol used to drive us doon there so grandma and pappa could get a poke when they were still alive. It's different going places in a car though. You dinnae notice how you get there as much. Then we turn the corner and I'm fucking lost. I dinnae ken if we're nearly there yet or no, not that it really matters as long as the bus goes back to Longstone. I just wish that fucking weirdie woman upstairs would get off.

There's this really heid-nipping high-pitched sound and I

realise the driver's trying to whistle. What a fucking awful racket. Jesus, why do all these cunts try to whistle? Sitting in traffic jams all day must make them go a bit mental. It's no the cunt that made a twat of me when I got on though, he must have changed buses to go and terrorise a new bunch of passengers.

Why are bus drivers always such cunts? Either they deliberately drive past when there's about twenty people standing in the pishing rain with their arms out, or they sit and play cards at the depot and don't turn up at all, or they let you on and give you grief or drive you mental with their awful fucking whistling or that *eeeeeeh* noise they make when they huvnae shut the doors properly. Why have fucking pond life like that in charge of barrie things like buses? See when I make a fortune with my computer games I'm going to buy my own bus and tank along Princes Street crashing into every cunt like I'm at the dodgems. These bus driver bastards are gonnae be dead.

We get to the end of the High Street and the holy willie finally gets off, still muttering her scary wee hymns and gies me another fucking evil glare. I check to watch she doesnae jump back in the out door and grab me from behind but she just walks off with her fucking bible open, mouthing away to herself. She should be in the fucking jail. I winnae get a 44 again in a hurry. They used to put folk like her in loony bins but now they just let them wander about the streets scaring folk shitless. I hope she's not still raving about when we're on the way back.

I'm still worrying about her, and thinking about the deformed guy and wondering if I havenae imagined it all 'cause it seems too frightening to have actually happened when the bus stops in the middle of fucking nowhere and the engine cuts out. Fuck, is this it? What a fucking shite-hole, he better no make me get off here. Surely he winnae?

The cunt does though. It's starting to pish doon now as well but he's chucking us all off regardless. Fucking Nazi. I beg the guy to let me stay on, tell him I'm going back towards Longstone, that I dinnae have a jacket and I point oot at the rain which is now fucking chucking it doon. He just blanks me till I stop pleading then looks really pleased with himself and tells me he cannae let passengers on for the return journey till he's had his break. Loadae shite. If mum wusnae so stupid I'd get her to write to the papers aboot it. Expose the bastards. The papers love aw that stuff aboot folk being cruel to wee kids or bairns getting shot or knocked-doon or dyin in fires. They'd probably pay her for a story like that and I could get ma picture took and a pair of Nike Air trainers. Scott and her would rip the piss oot of me if they kent I went roond on buses at night though. They wouldnae understand. I usually tell them I'm going roond to my pal Charlie's. They've never bothered asking where this Charlie guy stays or nowt, just as long as I'm no under their feet they dinnae care. Months ago I heard one of the inspectors calling this number 6 driver Charlie. That's who fucking Charlie is. I only remember it 'cause the guy felt sorry for me and gave me a bit of his piece when we got to the terminus. He probably got sacked for being too nice to passengers. Not like this cunt.

This place is the pits. There's just a big field and a car showroom and a wee half-deserted railway station. Why put a bus stop or a railway station in a place like this? What cunt would want to come here? I pace up and doon the shelter trying to keep warm and also 'cause there isnae anything else to do. There's just the car place but I hate cars – rich cunts drive them and they hold aw the buses up.

Mr smart-arse keeps giving me smug wee smiles as he drinks his lovely warm coffee out the lid of his flask and rams his puss with Kit-Kats. As he opens up his paper I take out my key and scrape National Kill a Bus Driver Day into the metal inside the shelter. Hopefully one of the sheep-shaggers that stay round here'll take it seriously and actually waste one of the bastards. You'd think it would happen all the time. Aw the poor cunts that have to use public transport, even old grannies, must have plenty reason to kill a few of the shitehooses every single day.

The cold's making me need a piss. Mum says my bladder's fucked. That's why I dinnae usually bring juice on ma trips with me. Sometimes I'm on a bus for three oors at a time. I couldnae hold it in that long. I pish like a leaky bucket at the best of times and I wouldnae like to have to do it on the bus. No like that guy did that time, clarty bastard. I wouldnae dae it in the shelter either 'cause it's bogging when you're waiting on the bus and there's an awfie smell of pish.

Instead I go into the field, behind a hedge. It feels really barrie as the pish steams onto the grass. Aaaaaah, yeah. I'm just savouring this feeling when there's a funny rustling sound that makes me jump and the last bit of wee wee splashes down my jeans as I hurry to zip up and get back to the bus stop. Shite.

I pull my jumper down to cover the wet bits. The bus is still no going. Come on you fucking arse-wipe! Some fucking tea-breaks they cunts get, eh? Laughing boy looks up from his paper to his watch to me, grinning away like he thinks he's God in his wee armour-plated box. I feel like decking the cunt.

My feet are so cold they're sore. Finally after what seems like about an hour the smart cunt starts up the engine and starts driving off, pretending he's forgotten me. I batter at the door till he lets me on. Fucking comedian, getting his kicks out of frightening wee laddies. Then the cunt asks to see my bus pass, gen, and checks my face against the picture. Fucking unbelievable.

No wanting to risk it upstairs in case that woman gets on again I go and sit at the back so I dinnae have to look at the cunt and 'cause I dinnae want him looking at me with his stupid grinning heid. Hot wind blows up through a vent in the floor and cosies me up a bit and the wheel vibrating under me feels barrie. The trip back's never as good though 'cause it's the one that always takes me back to mum and Scott. Do you think I'd get to stay in the hoose if they died? That wouldnae be so bad. Maybe I should gie them one ay they bad pies each.

Going back's like watching a video you've just seen in rewind. The bits at the end of the route you didnae ken on the way there seem like you've always kent them on the way back. Probably no one that lives in Edinburgh has been to all the bits I have. They dinnae ken all the funny shitey wee places I do. The roads are quieter now because it's getting late so the bus nashes through. I try to work out how far all these new bits are from Meadowbank where the real town starts.

From Eastfield onwards I sort of know where I am. Things look awfie different at night though and places seem to appear when you dinnae expect them to. Like I'm convinced Portobello power station moves about after it gets dark, it seems to get everywhere. Aw the lights across in Fife look barrie at night. It's like a whole other place just across that wee bit water. They should have a ferry going across from

Portobello, loads of folk would use it. You could get on free with a bus pass.

We're at the posh hooses again now. They've aw got floodlights and shit in the gardens so they can still show off how loaded they are when they're sleeping. I bet these places have games rooms and saunas and wee cinemas and stuff in them. They winnae have to play Sega on a shitey black and white telly. The folk that stay in them should let poor laddies like me go round for a wee shot, d'you no think? There's so many rooms they probably wouldnae even notice. I'd let poor folk come roond and play with ma stuff if I stayed in a big hoose like that. Greedy cunts.

Now we're back up at the poofy street again but I still cannae see any perverts. The papers probably just made it up 'cause everyone's getting bored reading aboot deid folk's greetin relatives and auld cunts dying fae bridie poisoning. It's too dark now to see if there's any shagging going on though. Maybe that's when they do it. Am gonnae get off here one night and see if any old poofs try and shag me. Aye right I will.

There's fucking coaches parked along half the street the night so they've probably aw been scared off. Hibs definitely werenae playing though so I dinnae ken what all the hoo-hah's aboot.

When we get up to Elm Row there's thousands of bingo-addict auntie beanie-types pouring oot the Playhoose. Some are going down to the coaches, or up towards the toon and loads of them are getting carted into ambulances and stuff and there's millions of mongols and cunts in wheelchairs as well, getting put away for the night.

Then I see this big poster of that creepy Cliff Richard cunt on the billboards ootside. I start laughing because I'm imagining that auld cunt shaking his knob aboot on the stage and all these spastics and auld grannies chucking their pishy knickers at him. It's fucking sad. I huvnae ever been to a real concert myself but I dinnae really fancy it. They concert videos are always shite. The bands aw play stuff no one's ever heard of that's on their CDs and when they do their chart ones they always ponce them up so you dinnae even recognise them. Crowds do ma heid in too, you always get daft cunts shouting out stuff they wouldnae usually shout out just so lots of people can hear them. Radges.

I'm fucking willing the bus to get through they auld cunts. Just knock them over you bastard! If we dinnae get up to York Place before them they'll start cramming themselves on, looking at people funny who dinnae get up to give them seats. Fucking cheek. They only have to pay twenty-five pence as well. They get on cheaper than any cunt but they still expect you to give them your seat, and they always seem to have that disgusting digestive-biscuits-in-their-knickers sort of smell aboot them. Some of these auld dears are minging. They should make the smelly bastards hing on the sides like they do in they Paki countries.

Ya hoor sir, there's no one at the stop and the bus just sails right past. It's fucking beautiful. I kneel on the back seat and give the vicky sign to them all until we turn the corner. It's a fucking hoot.

I'm still having a wee laugh aboot it to myself when we get up to St Andrew's Square and this strange-looking lassie gets on, all dressed-up like in really expensive model-type clothes, loadsae make-up but she's only aboot the same age as me. Dinnae get me wrong like, she's awfie nice-looking, sort of like Scully out of *The X Files* but just a wee lassie. The lipstick and adult clothes look barrie but kindae strange. She's got on one of they bubble jackets, the ones that are about a hundred poond, really fucking bright orange and these skintight black troosers and black high-heeled boots. The dead coolest wee lassie I've seen in ma puff. Every cunt's staring at her 'cause she looks so fucking cool, so fucking different. I start thinking that maybe she is just a toaty wee woman 'cause she's done-up so fucking nice, then I hear her talking to the driver and her voice is like a wee lassie's. I'm no able to take my eyes off her, I cannae help just looking.

I dinnae believe it, the cunting driver's giein her a hard time 'cause she wants to go to Balerno but she doesnae have the money. He tells her if she cannae pay the fare she'll have to get off. Poor wee thing cannae believe it and I think she's gonnae start greetin but she's wandering up the bus, trying to borrow her bus fare off folk. If I hadnae wasted all my money on that shite to feed my fat face I couldae gied her it but I got as much scran as I could. There's four-fucking-pound in my room as well.

This is terrible, aw they bastards are either ignoring her or pretending they've nae money or going through their pockets then telling her, sorry. Now she's talking to me. This coolest-looking lassie is actually talking to me but I cannae fucking help her oot. She gives me a look like she doesn't believe me, nae wonder after aw they cunts. There's always stuff in the paper aboot this sortae thing, aboot kids getting kicked off buses 'cause bullies have choreyed their fares and getting murdered and that when they're walking home. They cunts must aw ken what can happen. Surely one of them'll gie her the money? She cannae get off. The driver's refusing to go any further until she pays up or gets off. What is it? Aboot thirty pence or something?

I cannae believe this, I want to go and shake the bastards

until they give her the money but they're aw like fucking grown-ups so I just fucking sit there, useless, until she finally gives up and gets off. The driver shouts something after her I dinnae make oot and pulls away. As the bus moves down towards Princes Street I see her stopping this mawkit-looking old guy and I get this horrible creepy feeling that something terrible's gonnae happen to her the night.

A really panicky, scared sort of sensation is speeding roond ma insides. Why did I not get off and make sure she got home OK? I wouldnae ae minded walking aw the way to Balerno with her. It wouldae been fucking barrie. But she'll probably think I'm just the same as all these other greedy cunts now. I dinnae want her to think that, I really dinnae. Then my thumb's on the bell and I'm fucking ringing and ringing it but we're stuck at the lights beside the Waverley Market. I keep ringing, fuck. The driver looks oot from his wee secure box.

'I fucking hear you. The stop's along there, right?'

'Please mister, can you no just let me off here? Please? The traffic in that lane's stopped anyway.'

The cunt refuses though and when the lights change we're away past the Scott Monument before he opens the doors. I boot the side of the bus and gob on the windae as all the greedy selfish fuckers gawp oot at me. Then I just start running. Running like absolute fuck. The traffic's aw moving now but I just nash through it, squeezing between cars, almost getting squashed into the road by a huge fucking juggernaut, kicking aw the buses as I go past them but I just keep running and running and running till I get aw that sare-heided-cannae-breathe sortae way.

Aw I can think of is that lassie. It's like it was aw meant to happen and she was meant to get on that bus. It has tae be important if it's making me go radge like this. She cannae think I've let her down, she just cannae, whoever she is.

When I get up to the job centre I stop for a second and wheeze for breath and squint up St Andrew's Street for that bright orange jacket. I look in the doorways of aw the banks and aw up roond the square, over to the grassy bit then I go in the bus station and look along aw the aisles and the cafe and the alley that cuts up through St James Centre, even in the ladies' bogs but I cannae see her anywhere. Fuck, I keep going and looking at the same bits over and over 'cause she couldnae just disappear like that. No other buses have come doon this bit yet so she's here somewhere. Aw I can see though is folk with cases and studenty-type posers oot on the piss and boring posh cunts. I honestly feel like greetin.

After I've checked aw the places I'd already looked I walk along to the phone bit and throw myself onto one of the seats. I'm finding it awfie difficult no to cry now. It feels like the worst thing that's ever happened to me has just happened. I curl my toes up in my shoes to stop the tears coming but I really dinnae care any more if they do. Aw I care aboot is the sad look on that lassie's face. Why didn't I get off when she did? We could be walking back to Balerno right now, her safe, dead fucking pally. She'd have liked me if I'd helped her for definite. I really cannae believe she's gone, it feels like some cunt's died. Everything that's ever happened to me before this seems just silly all of a sudden, crappy in comparison. Nothing fucking matters any more.

As I sit watching aw the folk going past I hate them, aw of them 'cause I ken if they'd been on that bus they'd've ignored her too. I hate them 'cause they dinnae ken what I'm doing here, what I've just tried to do. Their lives are stupid, fucking selfish.

Ages and ages pass but I just keep sitting there in case she comes back. It's fucking freezing but I dinnae care. I was meant to help her like, I feel like the guy in *Terminator*, like I was just born to save her. Where the fuck has she gone?

Thinking of all the possibilities of what's happened to her, or if I'd got off the bus when she did or no spent all my money on sweeties and shitey salt and vinegar I dinnae even like, or if that bastard driver had just let me off when I asked him is making me feel sick. I just want to lie down and sleep here until she comes back. I'm scared to leave in case she turns up again when I'm gone. I dinnae even ken what time it is.

It gets later and later and I'm still fucking sitting there, no knowing what to do, just waiting as the place fills up with scary old jaikies and junkies and aggressive cunts pished oot their faces and I keep getting they bursts ae loud, angry-sounding voices seeming like they're getting nearer and nearer. There's hundreds ae reasons I should get the fuck oot ae there but an even bigger one to stay. Where the fuck is she? She shouldnae be alone in a place like this. I wait as long as I possibly can, till I really cannae stand it any longer.

As I slowly start to walk towards the bus stop I still keep looking behind for her. I'm still looking when the 44 turns the corner. For a moment I just want to let it go past but I'm freezing and still soaking from the rain earlier and I feel fucking useless. Like a fucking useless cunt. I just want to go to my bed and no wake up.

Getting on, I go upstairs hoping it's full of fucking psychos, hoping something awfie will happen. The bus speeds away like it's hurrying to get me away from it all. It feels like time is passing really quickly 'cause we're going so fast. Like it's getting as far away in time as it is in distance, like in science.

It's ten to twelve when we get to Haymarket. It must have been aboot ten o'clock when I first saw her. What was a lassie like her hanging aboot there at that time of night for? Sometimes it seems like nae cunt cares aboot anybody any more. The world's just full of sad folk wandering aboot on their own.

It's no until I'm walking up my street, looking at the neighbours' hooses, the shops and gardens and aw the poxy fucking things that huvnae changed since I was wee that I start to remember who I am. That anything had ever happened before tonight. I fucking hate this place.

Tomorrow I'll get a 44 again and look for her. I'll look every fucking night until I see her again and tell her I'm sorry. Fuck it, I'll wear a big jumper and my blazer so I dinnae even have to leave this time. So's I can just stay there and wait till she comes back.

There's no lights on in the house. I remember for the first time in hours that it's my birthday and for a minute I think they might aw jump out and say surprise when I get in. I couldnae really handle anything like that though. They're more likely to kick me aboot the living room anyway. There's nobody in. Mum's left a note pinned to the unit that says *In Ryries. Finish the cake.* Thanks a lot, I think. Thanks a fucking lot.

I check the paper to see if anything decent's on. Shite, I missed *The X Files*, but I cannae really be bothered watching telly anyway. I couldnae even concentrate to play Sega, even in colour. I go into the kitchen and eat a few cheese slices, then get a couple of Penguins and go to bed with that wee lassie's face like a Polaroid photo in my heid.

Of Cats and Women

SHE WAS SITTING in the car watching his house when she first saw his slut. They'd spoken several times but that was before her ex had gone ex-directory. When she used to phone after he'd first left, she'd hang up when the slut answered but soon rejected this silent endurance and let her have it a few times. It was her right. Let the bitch know what it's like to lose someone you've spent half your life with. She'd even looked up her thesaurus one night for further abuse to hurl when she ran out, but the potential ammunition she found depressed her. The words all sounded vibrant and exciting – harlot, strumpet, Jezebel – expressions that the cinema had turned from insults into sexual compliments.

It was after one of her more colourful monologues on morality and the slut's obvious lack of it that he'd changed the number. When sobbing, swearing and screaming down the phone left them unmoved she'd resorted to getting all biblical and raving about eternal damnation and the like. She wasn't a Christian herself but there were some wonderful insults to throw at slags and cheating bastards like them in the Old Testament. So when the verbal assaults ended abruptly, the emptiness suppressed since his leaving suddenly surfaced so quickly she almost got the bends.

His friends and relatives were hounded in vain for their new number. Personal mementoes from their marriage were posted to them daily, all desecrated in some way – wedding photos with female genitalia from porn magazines glued on where his face should be, old love letters he'd sent her with 'LYING CUNT' scrawled over every endearment, his Cup Final tickets shredded into confetti . . .

She started driving past his house in the hope of seeing him. When this proved fruitless she'd park on the corner of the street opposite, and sit watching for hours. On the few occasions she had seen him (he hadn't spotted her) she felt coy and nauseous, like she used to feel when she'd first fallen in love with him.

Although she'd always somehow expected the slut to be in her mid-thirties, the recognition was immediate and instinctive. It grabbed her the moment she saw the girl turn the corner and walk into his street. She looked no older than twenty. When he'd left she hadn't been able to think of how long it might have been going on. Now the question consumed her as she watched the girl stop by his door, pick up his cat from the wall and caress it. Suppressed sobbing clutched her throat and hatred thundered in her chest. She stared, transfixed with despair until the cat and its new young friend entered his house and closed her out. Starting the car, she drove off. Her vision was distorted by tears and an image of him sitting on the settee with the cat and the slut – so fucking revoltingly cosy it made her gag.

Nearing home, the anguish developed into unrestrained plotting. A skilfully contrived new plan was born that could be put into action while he was at work the following day. Invigorated, she sat scheming at the traffic lights until three young girls crossed the road in front of her, laughing and smiling with their perfect skin and taut little carcasses. A compulsion to suddenly accelerate was resisted with difficulty.

On arriving home, she depleted the Christmas port, plotted some more then went to bed. For hours the plan kept enlarging and exciting her too much to sleep. At 4 am she gave up trying, pulled a coat on over her nightdress and drove back towards his house.

From her usual spot on the corner of the street she could see the lights were out upstairs. Quietly leaving the car, she walked across the road and peered into the garden. Despite the lamppost's illumination she could see no sign of the cat. She tried meowing a couple of times but the ludicrous sound emitted was not sufficient to entice it. She returned to the car and sat watching the house. Were they at it at this moment? What little party tricks did she perform in bed to keep him so hooked? Images of them squealing together in elaborate sexual positions only served to deepen her melancholy wrath.

This ritual was performed for the next two nights with no result. On the fourth night his car wasn't parked outside. The cat looked on with indifference as she opened the gate. Approaching it warily, she began to slowly caress the warm fur. The creature responded, purring, rubbing itself against her, asking for more. She brusquely pulled it off the wall into a holdall, zipped it up and ran back to her car with the animal screeching and struggling through the nylon. Speeding back towards her flat, the adrenaline coursing through her system, she switched on one of the classical radio stations. Verdi at volume eight effectively quelled the sound of its wailing and she felt more in control than she had done in months.

The animal was left in the holdall overnight to prevent it running around the house creating havoc. In the morning there was no movement from the bag. She kicked it and felt the cat wriggling about as her foot made impact. How long would it be before he realised his precious pussy was missing? She unzipped the bag, expecting it to leap out and attack her, but it merely lay, blinking at the light, looking decidedly shell-shocked. There was a strong smell of ammonia and the lower part of its body was wet with urine. She flicked it hard on the nose to express her disgust.

In the bathroom, she plugged in the shower and switched it on. She didn't want the animal jumping on the furniture covered in its own mess but she remembered it wasn't too fond of water. Towards the end of their marriage she'd thrown it at him in the bath in the middle of an argument. It had made a hell of a mess but it was worth it. If he'd been seeing his slut back then he'd have avoided her for a couple of weeks after that one – that's for sure.

She pulled a scarf from her bedroom drawer and tied one end of it to the pipe in the shower. Returning to the living room, the holdall lay empty. She glanced around the room and began searching behind the furniture. Her hands began trembling with rage and her breathing quickened. Cushions were torn from the settee and thrown across the room.

'Come on . . . kiss kiss . . . come to mummy. Come and have some food you little bastard.'

She crouched on the floor, and squinted across the carpet. The door had been closed so it had to be in there somewhere. Then she saw it, curled into a ball underneath the bureau, eyes twinkling out at her. She smiled, her breathing loud and uncontrolled, pulled the shoe from her right foot and crawled towards it. It was right against the wall but if she lay on the floor she could still get a good swipe at it. A stiletto would have been ideal but not being the sort of woman to ruin her feet just so a man could get his jollies, a court shoe had to suffice. She prodded and clobbered at the cat as it backed further and further away from her. After a few minutes she didn't even know why she was hitting it, only that she didn't want to stop as it felt wonderful. Also, the idea that a perfectly aimed blow could kill it thrilled her so that every time she struck it she throbbed between the legs. The cat, unable to get any further away from her, began lashing out. As it shredded at her exposed hand and arm she felt justified in intensifying the beating. Suddenly there was a long, even, hissing sound. She pulled her arm out from under the bureau and peered in. The animal stared out, terrified, pissing on the carpet. She felt a strange sense of achievement, stood up, carried the holdall through to the bathroom and poured its ablutions from the night before down the toilet. There was no litter tray and it couldn't be let out so she'd just keep it in there until she got the information she required.

She moved the bureau, grabbed the cowering animal and forced it, scratching and hissing, back into the bag. Apparently they could survive for at least a fortnight without food so hopefully it would stop doing the toilet soon.

It was kept in the holdall for five days, only freed occasionally to have a drink or be tormented. On the third day it finally received its shower. The scarf was still tied to the pipe. Tying the other end to its collar she fired the spray of water at it as it slipped and struggled and lashed out in vain.

Another pastime involved throwing it about the house at different items of furniture to see if cats really did always land on their feet. Rather disappointingly this turned out to be the case but at least if it damaged anything in its doing so she had a further excuse to punish it.

As her treatment of the creature became more extreme she became increasingly aroused by it and obsessed with the idea of murdering the thing. The ultimate thrill, of course, would be for it to die of fright. To make something so scared that you actually killed it. Unfortunately though, this beast seemed pretty hardy and always found the strength to lash out just when her dream looked set to be realised.

On the fifth night he telephoned to tell her the cat was missing and ask if she knew anything about it. She remained calm and asked him why he thought she might know.

'Oh come on! Some of that stuff you've been sending us ... you sick bitch. Shouldn't you be seeing some-one?'

She didn't reply.

'Are you still there?'

'I've sorted it all out now,' she whispered but he continued talking as if he hadn't heard her.

'... and Karen said tonight there was a woman watching the house last week. No prizes for guessing who she might have been I don't suppose?'

Another silence. He began shouting.

'Jesus, won't you just leave us? Was eighteen years' misery not enough? It's finished, you know, over, can't you get that through your thick skull?'

Her fingernails pierced the skin of her palm.

'... and if you have Monty just give him back, will you? Have some dignity, woman. Or are you that desperate for the company?'

'I don't have your Monty. I told you. I've sorted it all out now. I won't bother you again.'

'Really?'

His tone was softening. He must be feeling guilty.

'No. Advertise or something. He's probably just run off somewhere.'

'I have. I put an ad in the ... you know. No, I've tried that.'

The arsehole. He knew he'd let it slip. She pretended she hadn't noticed.

'Anyway, I'm sorry and as I said, I won't bother you again.'

He didn't respond.

'Goodbye, Alan.'

He remained silent, but just before hanging-up she heard him mutter, 'I wish!'

Replacing and lifting the receiver she dialled 1471. As the voice informed her that the number had been predictably withheld she began to cry. Her tears were not the bitter, hurting kind of the past few months however, but tears of laughter and relief. He'd believed her and she felt omnipotent. She wasn't liberated from him but liberated from caring.

Running through to the bedroom she pulled the slip from her pillow, grabbed a shoe from under the bed then walked quickly through to the holdall, which was lying on top of the table in the living room. She unzipped it slowly and began caressing the cat's ears and neck. Though apprehensive at first the animal gradually began to relax a little. As she falteringly regained its confidence, she laid the open end of the pillowslip on the table beside the bag. Tickling its stomach she slammed the shoe heel against its head, grabbed it by the neck and thrust it into the case. She held it shut tight at the top, at first with a leg jammed and tugging in her fist, but manoeuvred it until the whole cat was lying on its back, enshrined in cotton. It wriggled violently and as the material strained in her hand, shockwaves shot through her body, making her gasp for breath. She walked across the room to the open patch of wall beside the door and smashed the bundle against it. The cat continued struggling so she continued battering the woodchip with it. It died very quickly but she continued whacking it until she could see blood on the wall.

Dropping the pillowcase onto the floor she looked out the window. When her breathing stabilised she carried the corpse, still in the slip, to the car, laid it on a black bin bag on the back seat then drove towards his house.

It was dark but the lights were still on upstairs. The curtains were drawn. She stopped in the middle of the street, carried the bundle out in front of the car, and tipped it onto the road. The body was still intact. Most of the blood must have come from its head which was caved in. Throwing the bloody cotton case onto the back seat, she got back into the car then reversed ten feet and accelerated over the cat. There was only a slight bump as she drove over its body but it was dead anyway. She continued driving in a straight line until she reached his local shops 100 yards away.

Taking a pen from the glove compartment, she walked over to the group of shops and scrutinised the small ads in the windows. He had a card in the newsagent's and the post office. She jotted down his new phone number, turned back down the street to have one last look at Monty, then drove home feeling like God.

The Initiation

THE FOG WAS sliceably thick and clung to them like wet clothes. A thin coat of condensation covered the park bench so that she and Jackie had to squeeze their bums together on the carrier bag they'd got the fags and juice in. Even the leaves and grass were damp although it hadn't rained for days. Lighting the first two Regals from the ten packet they stared in silence through their smoky breath as ghostly shapes dodged in and out the swirling pyramids of light above the tennis courts – jogging, walking dogs, running to and from unknown locations.

They laughed as a patch of sky above St Michael's kindled with a bang, reminding them of Miss Bennett's white, scared face that afternoon. A fortnight had passed since Guy Fawkes Night but the smells and sounds of treason lingered.

'A still cannae get over that shakin',' mused Jackie, sympathetically. 'She's had bennies before, like, but that was ootrageous. Single fare to the Andrew Duncan job.' She feigned an epileptic seizure for full effect.

Claire echoed her friend's hilarity but felt a private pity for their teacher. Setting the firework off in the classroom had raised her several notches in the estimation of the bullies she wanted so hard to impress, but something niggled her. When they'd seen Miss Bennett afterwards through the headmaster's door, crying hysterically and that weird trembling it was like she'd completely lost control. Claire knew she was responsible, though anonymously, for getting an adult in such a state and it made her feel great but awful at the same time.

Claire watched her friend sucking on a Regal as she rocked backwards and forwards on the bench, hugging herself, smiling into the fog.

'It was a cracker, Claire! Maybe there's hope for you yet.'

The slight accolade evaporated Claire's doubts and made her feel gloriously hard.

'It served her right. Fucking old bag,' she spat, relishing the feel of the bad word on her lips.

Jackie guffawed, repeating her friend's words in pigeon posh. 'Sorry, like. It just sounds funny when you say it, ken?'

Claire held the cigarette out in front of her, thinking how pale and lovely her hand looked in this light – almost like a statue. Jackie stamped her cigarette into the grass, then quickly dropped her head towards her friend and whispered an order.

'Hoi! Look down. Pretend you havenae seen him!'

'Seen who?' said Claire predictably as a tall, gangly youth shambled out of the gloom, grinning vacantly.

'Shite!' muttered Jackie.

The boy now loomed over them, beaming down, hands plunged deep into jogging bottoms.

'Whit yi up ti girls? It's a stinkin' night.'

Jackie scrutinised her shoes. Claire knew she had to get rid of him.

'We're having a gang meeting. We've got important things to talk about.'

The boy slumped down beside her, excited.

'A gang! A didnae ken yi wur in a gang, Jackie.'

Jackie looked at Claire and shrugged, willing her to elaborate on the lie and get rid of him.

'Whit gang's this then? Whit's it called?' he persisted, nudging Claire to respond.

She desperately clutched at a name she'd seen sprayed on a few bus stops.

'The SWP. You better not tell anyone though.'

The boy gaped at them, his mouth hanging open so his breath vaporised in the cold air.

'You must have seen it. It's written all over the place.'

He smiled, not really registering, and looked at her friend.

'Aye, brilliant, Jackie. It must be brilliant been in u big gang. Add love that. It must be brilliant.'

'Aye, Johnnie, it's brilliant,' said Jackie, reluctantly looking up from her shoes. 'Will yi leave us alone now?'

Johnnie stood up, embarrassed, and shoogled his crotch.

'Aye, awright girls. Al away, likes. Brilliant aboot yir gang, though.'

But he didn't go away. He stood shuffling awkwardly, hopping on one foot then the other, clearing his throat nervously.

'See ya then,' Jackie shouted.

Johnnie shut his eyes, screwed up his face and put his hands on his head. He let out a whine. Claire felt a less subtle approach might work.

'Look, will you fuck off!'

Johnnie ignored her, pointing behind them at the canal. His eyes remained shut as he continued his long, high-pitched wailing.

'What the fuck . . .' hissed Jackie, '. . . you're doing my head in.'

He began hopping again, still pointing towards the water.

'Mah hoose. Hiv yir meetin' in ma hoose. Yi cannae sit oot here.'

They both looked around but could only see the faint outline of the canal bank through the fog. Jackie looked back at Johnnie, gyrating on the grass to the sound of his own whining.

'A thought yi wir stayin' in the hospital. Wi cannae have oor meetin' in there.'

Her words seemed to please him.

'Naw, naw, no anymore. They said a kid go. Thir wisnae enough room for ais.'

'What about your mum?' asked Claire, slightly intrigued. Johnnie laughed as if she'd said something ridiculous.

'Nah, a cannae see her causey ma theivin'. A cannae help it, like. A just dinnae think. A kin git yi stuff though, fir yir gang, like. Biscuits, juice. If yi use ma hoose al make sure yi have biscuits.'

Jackie held up the packet of Regals.

'What aboot them? Kin yi get us them?'

Johnnie nodded his head enthusiastically and began jiving backwards towards the canal, beckoning them.

'Aye. C'mon. A kin get anything. That Paki disnae watch. He's ayewis on the phone.'

They followed him without really knowing why. He skipped across the bridge and disappeared through the gate at the other side. They climbed through after him, emerging on the steps that led to the boatshed. He was missing in the fog.

'Johnnie?'

'Aye, c'mon. It's jist doon here.'

Claire wondered if this was what her mother meant about

not going away with strange men. Johnnie was certainly strange, and a man, in his twenties at least, but he just had the brain of a wee boy. He just wanted to be their friend. It was sort of exciting now too. She grabbed Jackie by the arm and they hurried down the steps after him. He stood proudly beside a little dirty hut at the side of the boatshed.

'Wow, don't you get scared here?' asked Jackie, thinking the place looked like something out of a video nasty.

'Scared i what? Am no scared.'

'You're no scared i anythin', ur yi, Johnnie?' winked Jackie.

'No really. A dinnae like bein' high up, mind. That makes me feel a bit funny but no really. Am no scared.'

Claire found it hard to believe. The shed was so overgrown she probably wouldn't have noticed it if it hadn't been pointed out to her. A wonderful place for a gang hut, though. If only they had a gang.

Johnnie pushed the hingeless door to the side, they walked in and he pulled it partly over the doorway again. He switched on a strip light on the wall. Jackie lit a cigarette as Claire nosed around. It was pretty disgusting. A pishy mattress and ancient sleeping bag took up most of the space. What floor there was was littered with half-eaten tins of food, boxes, plastic bags, sweetie wrappers, various pages of newspapers and dirty magazines. Claire stared at a photo of a woman with her hand between her legs. It was funny-looking. Her fanny was like an overripe tomato that had burst and she had even fewer pubes than Claire did.

Johnnie was telling Jackie about things he could steal for them as she sat on the mattress and scanned his lovely home.

'Yid have ti tidy it up though. Before we could use

it, like. If yi kin get us they ciggies though, that'd be great.'

Johnnie bounded about, offering them both biscuits, giggling, trying to show them things.

'Oh a will, a will. I'll enjoy doin' it fir oor gang. I've nivir been in a gang before.'

Jackie looked at Claire.

'Who said yi wir in oor gang? Yi cannae be in oor gang jist like that. Yi can get us the biscuits and fags, like, but that's just so we use this place fir oor meetings.'

Claire sat on the mattress beside her friend. Johnnie started dancing around and whining again. Claire thought he might be quite nice looking if he wasn't a retard. Jackie held her ears.

'Stop that fucking racket will yi, Johnnie? Go ootside u minute and we'll see if we kin let yi in the gang.'

He hopped expectantly. She pointed at the door and he left them alone.

'OK, then. You started all this gang shite. Whit d'we tell him? U'd sooner sit here at night than freeze ma knackers off in the park or some shitey shop doorway, like.'

Jackie was right. They needed a proper place to go at nights. Neither of their houses were any good. Jackie came from a large Catholic family and shared a room with two of her wee brothers. Claire's was no good because her mum didn't like her hanging around with Jackie's lot anyway as her family were never out of trouble with the police. This place could soon be done up, in fact, Johnnie would probably beg to do it for them. All this and free fags! And all they had to do was convince him there was a gang. He was so easy to fool they could play it by ear. It would be a right laugh. They could have him eating out of their hands, and he'd supply the biscuits.

Jackie shouted outside for Johnnie to come in. He greeted them as if they were long-lost friends and immediately started dancing around excitedly, tracing invisible patterns in the air with his hands. The two girls sat together on the mattress like Mafiosi.

They'd agreed that Claire do the talking to start off with since the gang had been her idea.

'OK, Johnnie, we've had a wee talk and we're going to let you do three sort of tests before we can let you in the gang.'

'Whit? Like gettin' yir biscuits?' asked Johnnie, trying unsuccessfully to curb his excited dancing.

'...and fags,' added Jackie.

Claire took control again.

'No. The stealing thing you have to do anyway. That's going to be your gang role. Just like you have to keep this place clean for us.'

Johnnie's movements became less frenetic as he tried to concentrate on her words. He crouched on the floor beside them.

'Aye, a ken, a ken. Jist tellies whit ti dae, like.'

Jackie looked on with amusement as Claire continued.

'Right then, it's best if you do the three tests tonight, so you can start sorting this place out when we're at school tomorrow.'

'Aye, aye. Aw. This is brilliant. A cannae believe it,' he shrieked, jumping up and down on his haunches, clapping like a hysterical Cossack.

'OK, then. First we'll have to see if you're fit enough to be in the gang, OK? So you'll have to take your clothes off so we can check you.'

Jackie clucked in disbelief. Johnnie seemed to think this was a marvellous idea, however, which hadn't really been Claire's intention. He pulled off his T-shirt, sweatshirt and jogging top in one enthusiastic lump then started on his bottom half. They both looked on dumbstruck. Johnnie's breathing was heavy and excited. As the trousers passed his hips they gawped at the outline of his willie through the brown nylon y-fronts. It was gigantic, so big it stuck out the top of his pants. Claire let out a shriek of disgusted glee. Jackie almost choked with laughter, hiding her head behind Claire's back.

'Dinnae, dinnae, al be sick. Make him put it away!'

When they finally managed to curb their laughter and looked up again, Johnnie had taken his pants down and was standing tickling himself. Claire put one hand over her eyes, and waved the other in front of him.

'No, Johnnie, it's all right. That'll do now. Honest. You're really fi . . .'

Her words subsided into renewed hysterics as Johnnie pulled his trousers back up. Jackie fanned her chest melo-dramatically and rolled her eyes.

'Aye right, Johnnie. Very good. Yi'll hiv ti show it to Claire on her own sometime though. She'd like that.'

They exploded again and wrestled each other onto the floor as Johnnie stood smiling nervously, rubbing his chest. Jackie surfaced from the scrum first and held her hand up to get attention.

'Right, right. I'll do the next one, OK?'

Claire giggled back onto the mattress. She'd already thought of another task but she'd let Jackie go first. Johnnie was on his haunches again and she could still see the outline of the big hard thing in his trousers which made her feel pretty and powerful. Jackie was taking centre stage now.

'OK, the next thing is yiv goat ti get the gang name tattooed on yi so folk ken yir in the gang.'

Johnnie looked worried.

'Bit a cannae afford a tattoo. They cost loads, do they no?'

'Aye, loads and loads, and you cannae just walk out without paying either.'

Johnnie looked increasingly upset as his membership of the gang seemed to slip away from him again.

'Bit a cannae afford it,' he droned.

'A ken, a ken,' said Jackie, trying to stop him making that awful noise again, '. . . dinnae worry aboot money. Yi hiv ti do it yersell anyway.'

'Ooooh,' shrieked Claire in delight at her friend's wicked new idea. Johnnie's big daft mouth hung open as he tried to make sense of it all.

'OK. D'y hiv a knife or summat? Summat wi a sharp point?'

Claire bit her bottom lip in delight. She was feeling ecstatic with the badness of it all.

Johnnie was shaking his head, looking a bit overwhelmed. Jackie crawled across the room and picked up an open tin with its lid still attached then dropped it and came back over with a rusty tin opener, the type with the spike. Johnnie looked warily at the vicious-looking weapon in her hand.

'It'll hurt, will it no?'

'It's supposed ti hurt. That's why yi do it. If yi want in the gang you've got ti be able ti take a wee bit pain.'

She handed him the tin opener.

'Just write SWP on your arm. Quite deep so yi git a good scar.'

His mouth dropped open again.

'A dinnae ken whit that looks like.'

'S . . . W . . . P,' Jackie sniped, as if she were talking to a child.

'A ken, a ken, but a dinnae ken whit that looks like,' he shrieked, agitated now. 'A cannae read.'

Jackie tutted and asked Claire for a pen.

'There's one in there,' said Johnnie, timidly pointing at a cardboard box next to the mattress.

Claire crawled over to the box, rummaged around and pulled out the pen and some drawings. They were blue biro sketches of the canal, the park, Johnnie's room.

'Did you do these?'

Johnnie looked round to see what she was talking about then ran over and grabbed them off her.

'Please dinnae look at these, thir secret.'

Claire pushed him away, 'Don't wet yourself, I'm only looking.'

Johnnie relented but still took the drawings from her and put them back in the box. Jackie drummed her fingers on her thigh.

'Look, just bring the fuckin' pen o'er here, will yi? We dinnae want ti see your fuckin' drawins anyway. No secrets though, right?'

Johnnie cowered over, offered her his arm and looked away.

'Am no doin' it fir yi! I'll write it oan in pen and you kin trace it. Yi kin manage that, surely.'

She smirked at Claire, pointing at him and pulling faces behind his back, then slowly began writing in large blue letters down the side of his arm, 'I ... AM ... A ... SHITE'.

Claire started laughing again. Why were horrible things so funny? Jackie sat back and admired her art work then picked the tin opener off the floor and handed it to Johnnie.

'Right, jist trace o'er that. Deep, as a said.'

Johnnie began scratching at the first 'I'. Jackie stopped him.

'No, Johnnie, it his tae be a lot deeper thin that. It his tae bleed or yi winnae git a decent scar.'

He winced as he pushed a few millimetres of the spike into his flesh and let out a little squeal. The girls watched on, fascinated.

'An nae noise. Yi hiv tae show us how brave yi are.'

The top of the 'I' was bloody and brown from the rust on the tin opener. There were several breaks in the cut but it was still legible. As he continued, he had to keep wiping the blood from his arm so he could see the pen marks.

The girls were silent. Johnnie was determined but slow. His tongue stuck out between his teeth as he squinted at the deepening scar, breathing heavily in concentration. He had no look of pain any more, just the will to carry on. To please them.

At last he finished and wiped away some of the blood with his saliva on a bit newspaper. They all admired it. The breaks in the lines gave it a jagged, barbed wire look that was quite effective. Claire felt a bit guilty but still found it funny as she watched Johnnie staring down proudly at the words 'I AM A SHITE' sliced into his skinny arm.

Jackie stood up, moved the door and told them to come outside. She told Claire to rub earth into Johnnie's arm to stain the scar. The idea disgusted Claire but she didn't want to look like a coward so she led Johnnie outside. Yucking and screwing up her face, she pressed the soil into the gashes on his arm. Johnnie barely reacted as he was still transfixed by his new tattoo. When Jackie told her to stop she rushed over to the canal bank and frantically washed the dirt and blood from her hands, thinking about his next task. Yes, Jackie would love this one. She walked back over to them both.

'OK, Johnnie. Just one more thing you have to do tonight. Then you've passed the first stage to be in the gang.'

They all went back into the hut and she told him about the episode with the teacher and the firework that afternoon. They both hated the teacher as she'd tried to get Jackie expelled for getting into fights all the time. Johnnie told Jackie she was like his sister whom he didn't see anymore and he didn't like anyone who tried to hurt her. Claire said that the teacher sometimes hit Jackie and gave her bad marks just so she'd fail all the time. Johnnie started crying as they embroidered wilder and wilder lies about the schoolteacher.

Eventually Johnnie couldn't listen any more, he was so upset. He put his arms up over his eyes and sobbed. To block them out he put his fingers in his ears but he still sobbed. He hated the teacher too for the way she'd treated Jackie. He'd never met her but he hated her. He told them he had to go out to do the toilet, to be on his own for a few minutes. As he picked up some newspaper from the floor to wipe himself with, Claire grabbed him by the wrist.

'No wait, Johnnie. Don't waste it.'

He froze, rigid in her grip, scared of what they were going to make him do next.

'You want to get your own back on that teacher, don't you?'

Johnnie looked worried.

'. . . for what she's done to Jackie? You do love Jackie, don't you?'

He was getting all confused and anxious again and was having trouble speaking. A little squeak was all he could muster.

'You want to stop her being horrible, don't you?'

He began sobbing again.

'A want ti help. A really do. I want ti be in the gang in all but a dinnae want ti hurt anyone. Your gontie make me hurt her.'

Claire put her hand on his shoulder, trying to calm him.

'No, we're not. Not hurt her. Just give her a bit of a fright.'

He was wailing. 'Naw, naw, I winnae hurt anyone.'

Claire was getting impatient. He wouldn't even listen to her plan although he'd already stripped off in front of them and slashed his arm to pieces for the sake of their stupid make-believe gang. She looked at Jackie helplessly. She sat smoking, watching, tutting, then let out an exasperated breath and stood up.

'Johnnie!'

In the corner he stood crying, mumbling to himself. He looked down at the floor to avoid her gaze. Jackie walked over and tried to put her hand on his shoulder but he pulled away. She persevered until he slowly let her touch him, put her arms around him, cuddle him. Suddenly his arms sprang to life around her back. He squeezed her tight.

'I dae love yi, Jackie. Honest I do. It's no right to hurt folk though.'

Stroking his hair, she shooshed him down.

'It's OK. Dinnae get so worked up. We dinnae want yi ti hurt anyone.'

'Ma airm hurts, Jackie. It's really nippin'.'

Jackie circled his back with her hand like she was winding a baby.

'It's awright, Johnnie. Jist dae this one thing in will come back here in clean it up. Make it no sore.'

Letting go of her, he looked into her face.

'Really, yill come back wi me again?'

'Aye, of course. Yill be in the gang then, won't you?'

He smiled and sniffled and wiped his nose on his sleeve.

'Aye, OK, am soarry. Al dae it. I didnae mean it.'

Jackie gestured to Johnnie. Claire walked over cautiously, worried that one wrong word might send him into hysterics again. He smiled at her, snorting, apologetic.

'OK, Johnnie. I don't want you to hurt her. Just scare her a wee bit. Me and Jackie have both done it already.'

'What?'

She told him the teacher lived in one of the stairs round the corner. Number fifty-nine. All he had to do was make a mess on her mat, just to annoy her. She deserved it because of what she'd done to Jackie. They'd go with him. Then they'd come back here and sort his tattoo.

'What sort of mess?'

'Oh, you know. A jobby. Just on her mat. We've both done it. She's really horrible, Johnnie. You see, it's not hurting her.'

He looked at Jackie for reassurance.

'Then yill come back here wi me?'

'Aye, Johnnie, a told you we would.'

'Promise?'

'Aye. Look, it's gettin' late. Yill hiv ti do it soon.'

He picked up his clothes and pulled them on. They had to describe the stair to him. Just round the corner, past the fish shop, three stairs up. The blue door. He could run round the block. They'd go through the back gardens and he could let them in from the green. It would look funny if the three of them went in the stair together.

As they repeated the instructions to him, he grinned, getting into the adventure of it all again and sprinted up the steps at the side of the canal, disappearing into the fog. Giving him a minute's start, they ran up and through the park themselves. They saw Johnnie running like his life depended on it, his new-found enthusiasm making them chuckle as they jogged across the grass.

The teacher's garden was accessed through someone's drive, over a wall and through a couple of fences. Claire lived at the top of the street. Jackie had seen the teacher in her garden one day when she'd been stealing a T-shirt off a washing line.

Johnnie had already opened the door and was waiting for them in the garden when they got there. He was panting and excited like a big dog.

'OK, Johnnie. It's the last door on the top floor,' Claire whispered. 'We'll wait down here. Just poo on her mat then come and meet us.'

'How high is it? A dinnae like when it's high.'

The whites of his eyes glistened under the light from a window.

'It's no high. Yi dinnae need ti look down,' said Jackie, putting her hand on his shoulder to reassure him.

His neck was keening towards the entrance of the stair now. His tongue between his teeth again. He wanted to do it. He was ready. They pushed him gently along the passage and pointed up to the top landing.

'OK, just up there,' said Claire, barely audible, 'and remember what she's done to Jackie.'

'OK, OK,' he said, jumping quickly and quietly up the stairs two at a time.

'And dinnae make a noise,' whispered Jackie after him but he was already on the first landing.

'What's he like?' laughed Claire.

'Daft cunt!' said Jackie.

They walked into the centre of the stairwell and looked up. They could hear the soft smack of Johnnie's trainers on the steps. Finally he looked over the bannister at the top and smiled, then looked a bit queasy and whined. Jackie gave him the thumbs up as his face disappeared back onto the landing.

They listened as hard as they could. There was a gentle ruffle of fabric. Jackie grabbed Claire's sleeve in disbelief and amusement.

'It's his troosers. Listen. He's taking them doon.'

They listened closely again and could hear him squeaking and straining, trying to soil the mat. Jackie touched Claire's arm then tiptoed towards the main door of the stair. Where was she going? Weren't they going to wait on him after all? Jackie stopped the door with her foot, leaned out and pulled the bell at the bottom. Claire heard it ringing on the top landing. Jackie came running back into the stairwell, laughing quite loudly now. Claire gazed upwards with her hand over her mouth to stop the laughter getting out. Johnnie was pushed against the rail of the bannister, lying on the ground, wailing. She pointed upwards.

'What's he playing at?'

Both watched, bursting with amusement until the door opened. They didn't hear the teacher say anything but

Johnnie started squealing and stumbling and bashing against the railing, trying to stand up. His bare arse was pressed against the bannister. He was trying to back away but he'd forgotten to pull his trousers up.

Then suddenly there was a 'Whoop' sound and Johnnie was there, above them, flying downwards with his trousers around his ankles. It was like it was in slow motion. As they ran for the back door they heard a horrible, loud crunching sound.

They vaulted over the wall, through the hole in the fence, through the drive and sprinted across the park, not stopping till they were back at the canal. They both stood wheezing at the bench, hands on their knees to hold themselves up. Unable to speak, Jackie pointed across the canal.

Even when they got into the hut and were breathing normally again, neither of them spoke. They began cleaning up, collecting the old tins and papers and wrappers in the box with the drawings and dumping them all in the canal. As they watched Johnnie's belongings being slowly sucked down into the black water Jackie broke their silent lament with a flamboyant 'Whoop'.

Claire listened to her friend's laughter bouncing around inside the canal bridge. Her mind had gone completely blank so she wasn't even sure what was supposed to be so funny any more. But slowly she became infected by it and joined in. Laughing until her insides ached. Laughing because she was afraid not to. Laughing until she was sure she would never stop.

Tillicoultry/Anywhere

SEX WAS THE main problem between Tom and Christine. At the beginning of their marriage it had been a mutually enjoyable, thrice weekly diversion but now? Well, being a wife and a mistress was certainly not as they had described it in *New Woman*.

If Tom was a bastard the rest of the time or smacked her about a bit or took her for granted it would be far simpler. Then she could perhaps sustain her dissent long enough to actually do something about it. But the truth of it was he was so damned affectionate, loving even. Some women might even say she was lucky.

Tom thought he had been her first. When Christine had originally told him this she had honestly meant the first man she'd been in love with, the first one who hadn't treated her like shit. The further the truth had got from her, though, the harder it was to shatter his delusion and now, years on, that delusion was thus intact. It was such a big deal to him. That was why his current preoccupation with sordidness was all the more difficult for her to understand.

Looking at him it seemed inconceivable. A good three inches shorter than her, Tom could probably fit his entire lower body into one leg of her mighty jeans. For all his lack of height however he looked strangely lanky, his body never having seemed to fill out like it was meant to. The puny upper part looked like a coathanger with a shirt drying on it, his face was gaunt and angular, his legs long, bony, clumsy looking things.

Christine had fallen for him in the first place because she thought he looked like James Coburn. She liked James Coburn because she thought he looked like her mum's neighbour. She had liked the neighbour because he reminded her of her Latin teacher who'd looked nothing like James Coburn or Tom. Nevertheless this chain of attraction had always enforced the idea that Tom and her were just meant to be.

It wasn't that Christine didn't enjoy sex, she definitely did, but loving sex, sex that expressed real feelings. Not the base, twisted kind that was a thing alone unto itself, the kind that reminded her of the serial using she'd been given in her younger, sillier days. The older she got the more the things she'd despised in her youth became requisite to her – ridiculous things like security, stability, trust, consideration, moderation . . .

In the early days of their marriage it had been all right, she hadn't minded doing it three, sometimes four times a day – in the bath, in the stair, even once while she was doing the dishes.

After they'd found out they couldn't have children though, Tom had changed. It was like a bit of him wasn't there anymore although he never ever said how he really felt about it. Then he started doing daft amounts of overtime or bringing piles of work home or endlessly decorating just so he didn't have time to think. The trouble was, having taken on the extra work, it was impossible to get out of. During the brief hours between work and sleep that they had together, one of them was always knackered or they had money or the house to talk about or a fucked-up friend to support or a desperately ill parent to tend.

Tom, always neurotic about his sexual prowess, would resolutely force himself to perform every night. Lack of actual desire or inclination however meant that erections became increasingly difficult to sustain or indeed achieve and supplementary stimulus had to be resorted to. They started watching porn together. First it was soft top-shelf-of-the-video-shop-stuff, then the behind-the-counter sort, transgressing to videos from the boys at work, imported ones with horses and gang-bangs and handicapped people. Such things left Christine cold but seemed to help Tom who watched them as he tweaked desperately at his half-flaccid thing until it was half-hard enough to make an attempt at penetration.

Erotic episodes from his past (and imagination, she suspected) were also unearthed, recited, acted out. This, she found, turned her on significantly more than the horsey videos but the inevitable references to ex-lovers silently upset her and she constantly had to remind herself that he was with her now, not them. That was the main thing.

Then there were the fish net stockings and suspender belt that squeezed her pot belly into a painful, wrinkly ball, the see-through bra that made her breasts sweat and chafe, zip-open fluffy knickers that gave her thrush, spanking, tying-up, weeing on each other in the bath, basically any supposedly arousing thing he saw in a video or read about in one of his magazines.

The further they had to go for Tom to get excited though, the more unexcited Christine got about the whole thing. Before he had gone like this, when they were still able to have ordinary sex, she would fantasise about him being the plumber raping her or her packing him in and him kicking down the door and raping her. Now these things were commonplace, however, she had to think about him snogging her in the missionary position to make herself come.

And then he started on about it. On about catching his ex-wife shagging his best mate years ago being the horniest thing he'd ever seen. About doing it with another couple being the one thing he'd never done, the thing he wanted to do most of all. Trying to make out that if she wouldn't do it he'd think she didn't love him. Talking about it like it was a film he wanted to see that she didn't really fancy.

The inevitable unappealing factors involved in such a thing, however, paled into insignificance to Christine's central, unpassable thought – that he wanted to do it with a woman other than herself. She tried to tell herself that it was good he was being up-front, that he didn't want to go behind her back.

On top of all that though, he kept going on about her doing it with another woman. At a push she could perhaps do that for him, out of curiosity more than anything. Not that she had any leanings in that direction. She knew a few lesbians from the gay clubs she used to go to in her teens with her friend, Callum, but she had never been tempted. Besides, none of them had ever chatted her up. However, the thought of doing it with one herself was far easier to stomach than that of watching Tom doing it with one. You could have the odd sly fantasy about something like that but the reality of it would probably be horrible.

As they lay in their bed that night, he tickled his balls and heavy-breathed about it in her ear.

'Imagine me watching some strange guy getting torn into you. Imagine licking some woman's cunt while she sucked on my dick. What could be fucking hornier than that?'

Christine could think of a hundred things hornier than that but instead she just said, 'Aye, I'd like that.'

The next morning Tom brought her breakfast in bed for the first time in years. Getting in beside her, he fed her soldiers lovingly dipped in boiled egg. Letting her finish the toast he produced a *Forum* magazine from the bag he'd bought the eggs in. Thumbing through the back pages, chortling when he saw something rude, he squinted at the densely printed columns.

'See, most of them you either have to write or it's one of these 0898 numbers that keep you hanging on for ages. But there was one, hang on ... wait ... aye, here, see this one.'

Huddling up beside her again he pointed to an ad in the miscellaneous section squeezed between Jack Strap the Slave Trader and Mummy Hazel's Nursery for Sweet Helpless Big Babies.

'Attractive middle-class couple, M40, 6' tall, athletic, F33, 5'3" seek couples mid-thirties to share good food, wine and discreet fun. Tillicoultry/Anywhere but can travel/accommodate.'

'What do you think, cuddly-bun, will we go for it? D'you fancy it?'

Christine didn't fancy it in the slightest.

'We don't even know who they are. They must be a bit strange if they put their home phone number in a magazine like that.'

'Not at all, Sweet Pea. I can suss them out on the phone. If I don't like the sound of them I can just hang up. I'll do a 141.'

'And what if you do like the sound of them?'

'I don't know. There's no hurry. Just go with the flow. We could maybe arrange something for my fortieth, instead of a present.'

Christine picked up the newspaper and started reading it.

'Awe c'mon, babes, please. I just want us to have a good time. No pressure, honest.'

Squeezing her hand he planted warm little kisses across her knuckles, staring up at her Bambi-eyed, whining like a dog that wanted out for a crap. He was just like a little boy, her little boy. She loved him so much it was painful, she was enslaved by it. Damn it. Putting down the paper she stared at him, feeling trapped.

'OK, OK, you can phone through there and see what they say but I want to listen on the other line. We'll talk about it once you've spoken to them.'

Throwing the magazine across the room with a whoop he grabbed her, rolled on top of her, kissed her, squeezed her, rubbed the lump in his trousers against her. Just as she started to feel quite aroused he rolled off her and sat up on the bed. Taking her hand, he resumed the knuckle-kissing.

'I love you, bunny rabbit. I really do. That you'd do this for me, for a guy like me, it's just fucking amazing. I'm fucking lucky to have a nice woman like you. I dinnae deserve you.'

They deserved each other, pair of fucking numpties that they were.

'It's enough, almost, just that you'd do it for me if I asked you. It's enough in itself.'

It wasn't, of course. Jumping up he threw the phone from the bedside table onto the bed and disappeared through to the living room.

The number rang three times before it clicked and the whirr of an answering machine preceded a posh, firm male voice.

'We're out as usual. You know the routine. Talk after the tone and we'll call you right back.

'Bastard!' growled Tom, as the recording beeped for a response.

'Er, hi, hello, erm I'm calling about the ad, you know, middle-class couple, uh so if you fancy meeting up, oh, I better give you the number, erm 225 1268, oh that's Edinburgh 0141, no it's 0131, isn't it? OK, oh yes, I'm Tom and my wife as well. Right, OK. Sorry I hate these things.'

Running back through looking like someone had stolen his scone he stood in front of her, rocking from side to side in frustration.

'Fucking machine. I thought it would be them. Did I sound like a right arsehole? I'm awful on these fucking things.'

'I'm sure they'll call back anyway. It'll give us a bit more time to think it over.'

'That's what's fucking worrying me,' he sulked, grabbing the paper and stomping out the room.

By the time Christine had washed and dressed Tom had exiled himself in the garden where he spent the entire day weeding, cutting the grass, plastering the stone door-surround, avoiding her, sulking, trying to make time pass quicker.

With Tom still ensconced out the front she marinated the silverside, peeled potatoes, chopped onions and peppers and parsley, crushed the garlic, taking him hourly cups of coffee for which he could only manage a grunt of ambiguous appreciation.

Christine watched him out the living room window, brooding, throwing little tantrums at the lawnmower, smoking like a chimney. He could get quite silly about things.

The dinner was consumed in virtual silence. Christine had invented a new recipe with all his favourite vegetables and herbs but he passed no comment and left half of it. Later, as they ate their syrup sponge (another of his favourites, again no comment) the telephone rang. Clattering the dish on the table he lunged on the receiver, his face dropping from a Tony Blair grin to a Belsen grimace almost instantaneously. He brandished the phone as if he were accusing her of something.

'Fucking Sandra!'

Christine's friend Sandra was in hysterics. A neighbour had just informed her that her husband Jim had been spending his evenings in the phone box at the bottom of their street with the dog. Jim had denied everything and said the woman must be confusing him with someone else but Sandra said he'd started walking the dog in the middle of the night and could go out in a downpour and come back dry. At least Christine didn't have to worry about that sort of thing. Tom was maybe a pervert but he was a monogamous pervert. As she listened to her friend's monologue her husband paced around in front of her, eyes pleading for her to get off the phone. As if they'd call back that quickly.

They spent the evening in front of the TV, Tom sitting stiffly in the armchair staring intently into space. In the middle of *Dangerfield* the phone rang again. Tom's arms shot out in front of him but he resisted the urge to leap on it. After four rings he casually stood up and strode over.

'Uh huh, yes I did ... yes, hello, hello. Actually could you hang on just a second?'

Cupping the receiver in his hand he excitedly gestured towards the bedroom. Tiptoeing through she picked up the other phone.

'What was that?' the well-spoken caller enquired.

'I'm just taking you through to the bedroom for some privacy,' said Tom, his voice a few tones higher than usual. 'That's better, hi.'

'Hello, Stewart Rutherford here, we just got your message. Edinburgh, aren't you?'

'Yes, Baberton, do you know it?'

'We generally meet up in a hotel in the first instance.'

'Oh yes, of course,' Tom gushed, 'Whatever you think.'

'We're through in Tillicoultry, you see. Probably best we meet you for a meal. It's you and your wife, isn't it?'

'Yes, Christine.'

'OK then. A bit of a meal, get to know one another, take it from there, do you think?'

Christine listened in, absorbed and appalled.

'That sounds fine. It's our first time at this sort of thing so you'll need to tell us what to do, you know, I don't know what's the done-thing.'

'I don't suppose you're free tomorrow evening. It's just we both run to very tight schedules so it could be a while before we're both available again.'

Tom went quiet. Christine waited for him to come through and check with her.

'That sounds fine. We've nothing planned, I don't think. Excellent.'

What the fuck?

'Well, Edinburgh is probably the best bet. Anywhere you

might recommend? Preferably with a decent restaurant, save us going out?'

'I don't really know. There's the Barnton, I suppose. It looks all right. Save you getting lost on the one-way system in the centre.'

The bastard was arranging the whole thing. What the hell was he playing at? Christine ran through to the living room and tried to grab the phone off him but he pushed her away, holding her at arm's length.

'Yes, yes. I'm looking forward to it, excellent, ring us back if there's any problem, otherwise we'll see you then. We can't wait.'

When he finally put the phone down Christine, livid, raised her hands to launch into an animated objection but he pushed them gently back down to her sides and spoke in a calming, slightly patronising voice.

'It's OK, don't worry. It's fine. He's a nice guy, bit of a bloody blether but intelligent sounding. You'll like him, babes, honestly.'

'I can't believe what you've just done. *We can't wait!* We were going to talk about it first, Tom, remember? That's why I was listening through there, you know?'

'Aw, chill out, sweetheart, relax, eh. It'll be fine. You heard him. They were busy after tomorrow.'

'And you believe that, of course?'

'God, can't you just give people the benefit of the doubt? What's wrong with you?'

'I've not even had time to think about it. I'm really not happy about this. Can't we just leave it just now?'

Putting his head on her shoulder Tom nuzzled into her neck.

'I love you, fuzzy duck. I wouldn't make you do anything

you didn't want to do. You know that. We can just do it for the night out, you know, the meal and that. How many new people do we meet these days?'

Christine felt sick. This Rutherford bloke sounded thoroughly obnoxious. The whole thing was utterly absurd but she hated refusing Tom things, especially things that other women out there could do for him. Maybe she could get drunk at the meal. If she was pissed enough it might not be so bad. Couldn't she just shut her eyes and put up with it for an hour or so? It wasn't really his fault they'd been rushed into it. But he could still have come through and checked with her. Her mind flicked between envisaging the thing in a cold, detached sort of way, to the horror of them both having sex with some strange woman. Why could he not be obsessed with golf or cars like any other man? Even drugs she could maybe handle, but this?

Tom stroked her cheek and forced her to look him in the eye.

'It'll be fine, OK. Stop worrying. He's a copper for God's sake.'

'So was Dennis Nilsen.'

'Oh come on. We need a bit of adventure in our lives, don't get so wound up about it.'

'Ocht, but it's just such a weird set-up, meeting complete strangers and knowing you're probably going to have sex with them before you've even spoken. It's not natural.'

'Of course it is. Thousands of people do that every weekend. How's it any different?'

'Oh you know what I mean. It just seems a bit cold. Premeditated.'

Tom would have none of it. It would be fine. They would look after each other and have a whale of a time. He loved her. He really really loved her.

That night they made love like they hadn't done in months – slow, tender, doing it in all their favourite positions, downstairs kisses, the lot, and all the time Tom was holding back, prolonging it until the sheets were clammy and Christine's body ached for rest.

In the morning she was brought breakfast in bed again, this time scrambled egg, runny in greasy salty water with lots of white pepper, just the way she liked it. Tom went into town and bought himself a new shirt and pair of boxer shorts, glorying in the sense of occasion. After his shower he pranced through to the living room, striking poses, his tackle a painful-looking mass in his too-tight new underwear.

Having given up smoking two years previous, Christine finished the cigarettes Tom had been smoking the day before, then had to buy another packet. Though she tried to keep her mind off the fast-approaching evening it was hard to think of anything else. She was having flashforwards. The more excited Tom got the more apprehensive she felt. Having thrown up the scrambled egg mid-morning she stuck to cups of tea for the rest of the day. By mid-afternoon she was in such a state she had to take a couple of the Valiums Tom had been prescribed when his brother died. Within half an hour she felt slightly more 'couldn't-care-less-ish' about it all.

Tom was dancing about the house, fussing, flustering, suddenly hankering for the Paco Rabanne he hadn't worn since Christmas. Colliding as they crossed the living room he grabbed her and began mooning, crooning into her hair,

'Maybe I didn't love you, quite as often as I should, maybe I didn't hold you quite as often as I could . . .'

Christine joined in as she was feeling a flicker of wooziness from the valium.

'I really do love you, Chrissie-Pie, you're the most important thing in the world to me, you know that?'

Tom's eyes were watering in that way they did when he became overwhelmed by the sense of his own emotion.

'. . . and if you really want we can forget about tonight. It would probably be a laugh but if you really don't fancy it just say. I don't want you to feel obliged to do anything for me. I love you anyway.'

Christine couldn't believe it. The dread began lifting almost immediately.

'Are you sure? I just feel a bit scared about the whole thing.'

His face seemed to recede.

'But there's nothing to be scared about, booby, probably nothing will actually happen. We'll just go out and have a nice meal and a bit of a drink and relax. I really don't think it'll actually come to it.'

'People don't advertise in magazines like that for people to have dinner with.'

Tom picked up the *Forum* from the top of the speaker and pointed at the cover.

'It's not a porno mag, poopy-face, look. It's a journal of human relationships, serious articles and things, not bare fannies.'

Flicking through the pages to reinforce his point, the spread-eagled ladies advertising sex lines weakened his argument somewhat.

'Honestly, it's a middle-class sort of thing. You know how

repressed these public school types are. They just like to talk about it. That would be OK, no? Getting a bit gished and talking dirty for a while?'

Defeated again she slumped on the settee. Kneeling at her feet he kissed her knees.

'This is as far as we'll go, babes. This'll be the end of it. I won't ask you to do anything after this. We'll go back to normal, please, just a final burst before I'm totally decrepit.'

Christine couldn't listen to him any more. Locking herself in the bathroom she sat on the pan, whimpering. Why this? Of all things. She'd sooner he robbed banks.

Through the sound of her bubbling she could still hear him at the door, droning on about it, still trying to convince her. At times his selfishness could completely scunner her but this was particularly unbelievable. Pouring herself a bath to drown him out she squirted a few blackheads onto the mirror and gulped down another one of his Valiums. Few things in life were as reassuring as producing fields of white thread from one's chin.

By the time the bath was filled Tom had ceased his pestering and no doubt gone off to talc his new pants or comb his fucking hair again. Stepping into the water she plunged her arse in before her ice-cold feet had time to register shock. After the initial rush as the temperature took hold she gradually felt herself melting into the sweet, wet heat.

Leaning her head against soapy porcelain she simmered in the humidity, her mind emptying, the feeling of relaxation slowly
consuming
her.

Amidst the whirring air vent and steady burrrrrrrrr of the cistern there was a tangible silence.

Christine basked in it, opening and closing her legs until ripples of water massaged her sides.

Then, into the midst of her glorious isolation crept a conflicting sound, like the start of a dream. From distant wailing, as she directed her hearing, it clarified until she realised it was a voice. She tried to hear beyond the cistern and vent. Singing. A man singing through the wall in the next house. A sweet, clear voice. It sounded like an old Irish ballad, definitely familiar but different somehow.

'Life is a mys-ter-y everyone must stand a-lone . . .'

A beautiful sweet male voice, no accompaniment. Like an orchid in the snow.

'. . . I hear you call my name and it feels like . . .'

'Ho-ome,' the voice in her head duetted with the faceless singer. My God, this was completely unbelievable. This was 'their' song. The one she used to play over and over when she was getting ready to go out with him in the days when she still used to put on a full face every time they met.

'Like a dream, no end and no beginning . . .'

It was almost as if she was imagining it, that song, with a man singing it.

'You're here with me it's like a dream, let the choir sing . . .'

The improbability of it all afforded it all kinds of significance in her head. It was a divine sign of some sort. A little confidence-bearing symbol to make her go through with tonight. A little reminder of why she was even willing to contemplate such a thing.

When she recovered from her epiphany she was alone again with the cistern and the vent and a feeling of having been physically shaken. Looking around the bathroom she expected it to look different in some way but she could detect nothing. All that had changed was her frame of mind from despair to something akin to Dunkirk spirit. Enlivened she soaped and rinsed vigorously, humming the song to herself, happy like a fool.

Afterwards, as she rubbed the thick, soft towel across her shoulders and back she watched the steam rising from between her legs. She'd never noticed that happening before. It looked obscene, like something out of one of his videos but it made her feel strangely sexy. Shouting him through the door to make her a cup of tea she cleansed and toned her face until it was as tingling and alive as she herself now felt.

Christine always felt better after a hot bath. Whether it was the shedding of a few layers of dead skin or just the general feeling of being cleansed and fresh, she always felt rejuvenated afterwards. Massaging moisturiser into her face, she stared at her reflection in the cloudy mirror. What she saw pleased her. It was good to be thirty-five and still look like this, still look young. Ready to take on the world she unlocked the bathroom door. Tom stood behind it with her cup of tea and a look of extreme apprehension.

'You had me all worried, baby cakes, how are you feeling?'

'I'm fine. Look, Tom, I'll go tonight for you, but this is as far as we'll go, really. You have to promise me that.'

'Yeah, of course, definitely. Don't worry about it. Are you absolutely sure, snuggle pup?'

'Yes, just stop going on about it will you or I'll probably change my mind again.'

Delighted with her new-found assertiveness she blew it by wiggling her chin and doing fish-eyes at him.

Shadowing her into their room, Tom sat on the edge of the bed, watching her putting her face on, egging her on to be a bit more daring than usual. Her cosmetic procedure had remained basically unchanged since her teens but tonight she made the eyes much darker than usual until they looked like lights at the end a tunnel. The lips she painted a dark rim around to enlarge and her usually blotchy complexion was honed to a smooth, fleshy ivory with a generous helping of foundation and powder.

'Whoargh! I'm getting a willie-twitch just looking at you, hot pants.'

Christine could understand what he meant, so impressed was she with the repair job she'd managed to do on herself.

While Tom shaved Christine rummaged about in the wardrobe, despairing at how long she'd had most of the clothes that inhabited it. Eventually she settled for the little black number she'd worn on the night she'd pretended to be a wanton hitchhiker for him. Tom loved that dress because he thought she looked really whorey in it. She supposed that was a compliment of sorts. Manoeuvring herself into it was like trying to stuff a potato into a condom but once the struggle was over the sensation of it clinging to her made her feel decidedly raunchy. A pair of 20-deniers were chosen above stockings since the dress was indecently short and tights tended to curtail any involuntary wobbling. Walking into a spray of Givenchy she admired herself in the full-length mirror, strutting through to join him in the living room.

'Wow wow wee!' he roared, his eyes bulging and face contorted into a libidinous gurn. His exaggerated expression made her cringe but she was pleased with his response regardless and lapped up his enthusiasm, confident as she was that she looked her absolute best.

Tom suggested they arrive at the hotel early to acclimatise and have a few drinks to loosen themselves up. Christine sensed that he just wanted to get there before she had time to change her mind again. He preened at himself in the mirror, pulling his jacket sleeves, looking with concern at the back of his trouser legs.

'I ought to get a new suit. This thing makes me look awfie skinny. I don't think it's quite right.'

It made him look skinny because he was skinny, what did he expect? Disappearing into the bedroom and shutting the door as if she was that desperate to see what he was wearing, she heard the wardrobe being rifled as he muttered and cursed to himself. Eventually he re-emerged in the black trousers she referred to as 'his second home', the new white shirt, Rangers FC tie and burgundy leather jacket, honking of Paco Rabanne. Performing to the mirror again he pulled at his collar, tightened and loosened his tie a few times, messed his hair, combed it then messed it again. For all the hours Tom spent fussing over his hair it always looked like the hairdresser had a spite against him. Tom, however, thought he looked marvellous.

'This is better, joob-joob, don't you think? More of a classic look.'

'Yes, love, definitely. The classic look.'

Poor man. Oh well, at least they both thought he was gorgeous.

The drive from Baberton to Barnton only took a few minutes. As usual they took the car because Tom insisted on driving everywhere. The taboo surrounding drinking and driving had never impacted on him as he always insisted, rather missing the point, that he felt more in control behind the wheel when he had a drink in him. This was confounded rather by the fact that he'd been stopped a couple of times but had never been charged.

He had been right though. It was good to get your glad rags on once in a while and have a little adventure. The smell of Givenchy and Paco Rabanne mingling with the car smell was one she always associated with them going out for the night. If she shut her eyes she would still know they were dressed up and on the way out. This was what they smelt like.

The bar was practically empty. A businessman on a mobile, an elderly couple, a group of student types speaking German. He ordered a couple of vodkas and they sat in a little alcove in the corner of the bar away from the others and with a good vantage point for the door. Tom frowned at his change.

'Four-fucking-sixty for two vodka and tonics, fuck's sake. We'll share the tonic next time. Let them buy it when it's their round.'

Christine turned to castigate him for his stinginess but he was grinning and wagging his index finger at her.

'Hah, nearly got you. Nee naw.'

He drummed a rhythm on the table and did snare drum noises with his tongue, eyeing around the bar.

'What are you thinking?' she asked.

His eyes twinkled with mischief.

'What'll you do if I fancy her?'

'What'll you do if I fancy him, like?'

Tom gave her a hurt look.

'Aw you won't, will you? What if his willie's bigger than mine? Will you pack me in?'

Poor thing. He had to be constantly reassured about his penis, so proud of it was he. Many of their little games involved him flashing it at her – in the supermarket, in crowded pubs. When he went to visit her at work sometimes he would sit opposite her desk with it in his hand. This was probably what tonight was all about. Any excuse to air his manhood.

They had another couple of drinks each, sharing the tonic, staring expectantly at the door. Tom kept checking his watch.

'They're twenty minutes late. Do you think we're being stood up?'

Christine's hard-won enthusiasm was waning and she was starting to hope they had been. She had peaked earlier after the bath and didn't have as much peak in her as she used to.

'It's only twenty minutes. Ask at reception if they've checked in.'

Tom was getting flustered.

'Give them till half past. If they're not here by half past, they're taking the piss.'

So they sat for another twenty minutes, watching the door. Not speaking to each other any more, just anticipating. Although she partly hoped they wouldn't turn up, on the other hand she wanted to get it over with and out his system.

Tom rat-tat-tatted his cigarette packet on the table in agitation.

'Bloody hell. I'm starting to go off the boil here. I'm really starting to get pissed off.'

'I've told you. See if they've checked in. Get them to buzz the room. If they're not here we can do something else, since we're all dressed up now.'

'If we've been stood up I won't be in the mood to go anywhere. This is fucking ridiculous.'

'Oh don't be so pathetic. Ask the bloody receptionist.'

He studied his watch as if it might tell him what to do next.

'I don't know. I don't want to seem desperate, you know?'

And phoning complete strangers in sex mags to have sex with you and your wife wasn't desperate? Why did men make these massive dilemmas for themselves out of nothing.

'Maybe they're sitting up in the room in the nude. Maybe they're just waiting for us to let them know we're here.'

'No,' he snapped. 'He definitely said they'd meet us in the bar.'

'I know but you could have got the wrong end of the stick. It has been known . . .'

Tom looked at her accusingly.

'You suddenly seem awfie keen. You've certainly changed your tune.'

Oh for God's sake, she couldn't win. He was really starting to annoy her now.

'I just like to know what I'm doing. I am most definitely not keen in any sense of the word. I'm here to keep you happy, that's all. Be certain of that.'

Sensing she was cooling to the idea again he finally got up and went to reception. When he returned he was grinning again and gestured her to finish her drink as he drained his own.

'They have checked in but they're not in their room. The receptionist's going to call them. She says they must be in here somewhere, they haven't handed in their keys.'

Christine stood squirming beside him as the receptionist bellowed over the tannoy.

'Could Mr and Mrs Rutherford, room four, come to reception please.'

How discreet. Meeting a couple of perverts for a liaison and announcing it over a loud speaker.

The elderly couple who had been sitting in the bar approached reception. Tom moved out the way, eyeing all the points they could possibly emerge from. The elderly man took his hand and shook it, fondling the knuckle.

'Stewart Rutherford. Lovely to meet you. This is my wife, Liz,' he said, gesturing to a ruddy-faced, very overweight woman in her fifties who gave them both a warm but sexless smile. Christine's breathing stopped for several seconds. Tom became animated and wouldn't shut up but looked like he'd just been given some very bad news.

Awkward introductions exchanged they made their way through to the dining area. Stewart instructed them all where to sit. Christine felt embarrassed about the whole thing and couldn't bring herself to even look at the pair of them, instead assuming an air of being utterly engrossed in the menu. My God it was expensive. Why could they not have gone to a nice Indian or something? You always got ripped off in these hotel restaurants. How would they go about paying the bill? She'd prefer to know how they were paying before she decided what to order. If the Rutherfords were paying she'd have the loin of pork. If they were going Dutch she'd splash out on the monkfish tails. If Tom and her were expected to pay she wanted back home to the scraps that they'd picked at the night before.

Stewart was still hassling them for their orders as he refused to pick the wine until he knew exactly what everyone was eating. Christine under duress plumped for the pork to be on the safe side. It was the cheapest main dish on the menu but was still about twice the price it would cost her to prepare it for the four of them. Christine loved food, but eating out really stuck in her throat as she always sat working out how much she could cook the same thing for herself.

The inhumanity of it all never failed to put her right off her dinner. She also prided herself on being able to calculate the price of her shopping as she placed it on the conveyor belt in the supermarket and was generally within ten pence. Paki grocers were another matter of course.

Stewart was still making a song and dance and encore about the wine list, reading out the names in a loud voice, just basically showing off his immense knowledge.

'A Macon Rouge? Oh not with pork, for heaven's sake. Oh look Liz, they have a 1993 Chateau Meaume, my fruity favourite, we simply must. Perhaps with a little Bairrada Branco for the salmon?'

Tom was nodding and smiling away like he knew or cared what this old poser was gibbering on about. It was something that really annoyed her about him, his misguided sense of class. It didn't matter how decent or intelligent or kind people might be, there were only two factors that decided whether they were worthy of Tom's attention – money and lodge membership. Stewart seemed to fulfil both these criteria hence Tom was in serious fawning mode.

Stewart gave the waitress the order in every sense of the word. God, Christine hated people like him. People who were rude and self-important with waiters and shop assistants. People who grasped at any opportunity to exert their delusions of superiority over others.

The girl returned with the wine and defiantly uncorked it an inch or two from the awful Stewart's ugly head. Grotesquely skooshing it round his mouth like Bisodol he swallowed hard and screwed up his face as if he'd been sooking lemons.

'Ih, it's very bitter. How has it been stored?' he interrogated the hapless waitress who at a probable £3.00 an hour couldn't give a shit.

'I can check if you like, sir. Or perhaps you'd like to try another?'

Christine was cringing. Stewart's wife was watching him utterly mesmerised as if she'd maybe just witnessed him healing a dozen lepers. Tom's forehead was perspiring and large flowers of sweat were blooming on the underarms of his shirt. He just wanted another drink. Unaccustomed as he was to drinking anything that didn't come in a pint glass (the vodka earlier had been one of his attempts at 'class') he was necking it back. Two visits to his lips was the greatest chance of survival a glassful had. Christine watched on thinking 'there goes another £2.10' every time he took a slug. Bloody ridiculous anyway spending all that money on a few bottles of vino collapso you could get change from a fiver for in Safeway's.

Stewart gallantly agreed that they would suffer the bitter wine. Who decided he would do the Egon-fucking-Ronay bit anyway? As this red-face progressed Christine kept noticing Stewart trying to catch her eye. She found it comical that this extraordinarily unattractive pair of oldies could actually think they were on a promise. It was sad really in a disgusting sort of way. An escape plan was yet to be devised but she would work something out. There was no question about that.

Liz stared at Christine and Tom with a glaikit look on her face.

'Stewart's very fussy about his wine. I suppose the more you know about something the fussier you tend to be.'

Christine almost got the dry boaks.

'I never bother with the names, I just go straight to the alcohol content. If it's more than 12.5 it's a good wine, if it's less than 10.5 it's a bad wine, if it's Liebfräumilch it's no' a wine at all,' chuckled Tom.

Stewart guffawed falsely, Liz gave Tom a look of pity which made Christine want to smash her in the face. Instead she took a gulp of the bitter wine which tasted beautiful. Stewart leaned back in his chair theatrically, smirked at Tom and made a farty noise with his lips.

'Yes, we noticed you both when you first arrived. You did look a bit expectant but you weren't really what we were anticipating so we thought we'd wait and see. What line of work did you say you were in again?'

'Computers. I sell computers.'

Stewart nodded his head in silent contemplation. Liz touched Christine's wrist to get her attention. Christine shuddered and reached for the glass to escape her.

'Yes Christine, Stewart thought it might be you but we weren't expecting you till a bit later.'

'Or do you like to be unfashionably early? Unorthodox types are you?' and he roared with laughter again. Christine wished she found him as amusing as he found himself. She'd be pishing herself if she did. She attempted a put-down but it came out shite.

'We needed some Dutch courage. We don't actually make a habit out of this sort of thing.'

'Nor do we dear, nor do we,' reassured Stewart, 'we already have a network of couples we've been seeing for years, you know, individually or in groups.'

'We just thought it was time to give a few fresh faces a chance,' squeaked Liz as if she was talking about a Salvation Army fund raiser. Tom was almost drooling in contemplation. It sickened her.

'So there's quite a lot, you know, of this sort of thing about?'

Liz giggled in her dulcet fingernails-down-a-blackboard

way and made a hey presto hand gesture to Stewart, Delphi Oracle of suburban wife-swapping that he was.

'Oh most definitely, Tom, you'd be surprised. I obviously don't want to go into too much detail until we know each other a bit better but I will say its not just a seasonal interest in William Wallace that brings visitors to the Stirling area these days.'

Christine actually managed a little giggle as the waitress arrived with the starters. She was resentfully extra-attentive, probably in fear of lashing out if the arsehole started again. Refilling the glasses she asked if there would be anything else. Stewart dismissed her by nodding his head and pointing behind his shoulder. The waitress remained stony-faced but caught Christine's eye. Christine nodded her head then looked into her broccoli and stilton soup with croutons.

Left alone Stewart recommenced. As he camply picked at his chicken livers he looked Tom earnestly in the eye.

'We have about thirty people in the Stirling area alone. Usually there'll be a group of about six couples and we just take it in turns to host parties.'

'What, you mean like orgies?' mumbled Tom through a mouthful of prawns, tomato mayonnaise appealingly adorning his top lip.

Stewart looked around self-consciously and lowered his voice.

'I suppose you could look at it that way, but it's a lot more sophisticated than the usual communal bump and grind, you know, live shows, games, that sort of thing.'

'We have an excellent version of charades,' exploded Liz, brimming with fundamentalist verve.

Tom whooped with laughter and looked at Christine in a

how-about-these-guys sort of way. She had to close her eyes to block out his sycophancy.

'Wow wow wee!' he exclaimed wildly once he'd swallowed his prawns.

'It's a social thing too, Tom, that's the great thing,' encouraged Liz, 'you know, a few nice bottles of wine, quiche, pavlova, a fondue . . .'

This couple were ludicrous. Christine was a heathen but she was sure that the sexual act had not been designed with this sort of thing in mind. She couldn't let them think she was taken in by this crap.

'And what about your sex life in general? How is that?'

'I don't really think that's any of our business, booby joe,' whispered Tom.

'No no, Tom, it's all right,' Stewart interjected, completely unperturbed. 'In answer to your question, my dear, our sex life is absolutely wonderful simply because this is our sex life. Sex is a beautiful thing which you shouldn't waste by attempting when you're tired or not in the mood.'

'You really think so?' said Tom, onto something.

'Oh definitely, limiting sex to our little get-togethers is excellent time management and it means the get-togethers themselves are all the more enjoyable. Everyone needs a little carrot to dangle in front of them.'

Christine spluttered. The insightful Liz elaborated.

'Imagine if people gave you presents every day of the year. Christmas wouldn't be half as exciting, don't you think!'

This pair were emotionally retarded.

'Personally Christmas ceased to be something I got excited about when I was about seven years old.'

'Well I must say I feel sorry for you, however, I think it proves our point,' said Stewart.

'Oh yes, you've certainly got me beat with a strong argument like that,' spat Christine, thrusting her glass out in front of her. Tom frowned at her as he poured.

'Calm down, honey pie. What's wrong with you?'

Christine grabbed her glass back, took a slug and folded her arms into a huffing position. Tom immediately turned his attention back to Fred and Rosemary.

'I'm very sorry. Please excuse her. It'll be hormone replacement therapy for Christmas I think, anyway, back to these parties. What are the folk like? Obviously respectable people like yourself?'

Christine exhaled dramatically but was immediately drowned out by the gushing Liz.

'Oh Tom, you wouldn't believe it – doctors, policemen, advocates, teachers, intellectual lorry drivers. People that work in stressful environments. People like you and me.'

Tom was utterly enthralled. Christine was thoroughly appalled.

'And it's not a bit awkward like, trying to get these things going? How do you decide who goes first?'

The waitress returned to clear away their starter dishes. Tom looked irritated at her intrusion. He was champing at the bit. Christine beckoned to the girl.

'Excuse me, could you possibly find out if my pork's been prepared yet?'

'Oh yes, madam, it should be with you in a few minutes. Was there a problem?'

Too late, dammit. Her appetite had vanished. She just wanted away from this shit.

'No, thanks, that's fine, great, thanks, thanks very much.'

Christine wanted her to know she wasn't like Stewart but the waitress seemed equally unimpressed. Tom was looking at her a bit concerned but as soon as the girl disappeared he was all over the Rutherfords again.

'So what, does somebody just strip off and say "come on then", or is it a names-in-a-hat sort of thing?'

'No no no, Tom, we're talking about a very informal, very relaxed situation here. It's an anything-goes environment so if you're all broadminded consenting adults there's absolutely nothing to be nervous about.'

They ought to be fucking locked up, thought Christine. Liz started up again. For a beaten-down little short-arse she certainly had a lot to say for herself though she was rather Ernie Wise to Stewart's Eric Morecambe.

'And as Stewart said earlier there's all sorts of activities to loosen people up.'

'Such as?'

'Well, maybe we'll have a bit of a floor show, you know. We had one of our neighbours hoisted onto a Perspex pyramid her husband had designed, you know, full harness and everything? She had over a hundred orgasms.'

'And who told you this?' sang Christine, unable to suffer this nonsense in silence any more.

'She said so herself,' said Stewart defensively. 'You see, Christine, it's not all tits and ass and cheesecake. You can even apply basic principles of engineering to it. Sex is much more multi-faceted than people often think.'

Tom wasn't finding this line of conversation as interesting.

'Anyway Stewart, back to these floor displays. This sounds really amazing. What sort of things are we talking about here?'

'Oh all sorts of things. We'll maybe watch a video one of the couples has made, or about six of the group will start a little performance to get us all in the mood, you know?'

'And we try out new sex toys,' said Liz, the words not quite gelling with the face they were coming out of.

'And we exchange magazines, videos, get notes of things on the Internet. Swinging is international. Obviously though I can't go into too much detail on our first meeting.' He glowered across at Christine. She glowered back.

'Yes, leave the sacrificial lamb for next time.'

'Ah yes, the lamb, the hazelnut and orange stuffing looks exquisite,' blanked Stewart as the waitress arrived with the main courses. Tom turned to Christine as they were being served.

'What the hell is your problem?'

Christine gulped down her wine defiantly and proffered her glass again. The waitress summoned the waiter to open the other bottle.

'You've had plenty. Don't have any more, right. Stop making an arse of yourself, OK, just sort it out!' He turned back to the Rutherfords. 'Honestly, I've never seen her like this before. I don't know what's wrong with her.'

'Lack of discipline,' said Stewart, sounding like Leslie Phillips, slimy bastard.

The waiter schlooped the cork out of the bottle and filled Christine's glass. Liz looked over, confused as to how anyone could possibly be unpleasant to the wank she was married to.

'Do you want to pop into the ladies' for a little chat, dear?'

'Certainly not!' Christine growled from her pork. Jesus, the nerve of the woman. Speaking to her like she was some silly wee lassie who's had a few snakebites too many. Tom was gesturing towards the toilets, trying to get her out the way. It pissed the hell out of her. Siding with these Stirling sickos after all the shite she'd put up with for him, like their feelings were more important than hers.

'I'll eat my overpriced pork if you don't mind,' she snapped, slittering the meat around in its Calvados and apple reduction with a lump of frustration swelling in her chest like couscous.

She could see Liz staring across at her creepily, out the corner of her eye as the two men isolated themselves in conversation. Tom had his back to Christine, his dinner unviolated beside him like a prop.

'Do you get much of a response, you know, when you advertise in these magazines?'

'Oh yes, definitely, very much so. We couldn't possibly follow them all up though. We are extremely busy people.'

'It was just so lucky you phoned at just the right time,' said Liz, looking at Christine and adding '. . . well maybe not the right time exactly but you know, we were all available.'

Christine tried not to listen, it was just winding her up. She chewed on a tiny piece of pork that just refused to go down as the voices droned on. Her mind played over all the ridiculous things she'd subjected herself to for him over the past few years, the vulgarity of it all. Of stockings that had given her nappy rash, of standing around Waterloo Place in the pissing rain in the middle of January fighting off jaikies while she waited for him to turn up and pretend to be a punter. Of all his friends who'd she'd made an extra effort to make like her because she was 'Tom's wife' and he wanted them to like her, only to have him offer her for sex to them on the understanding he could watch. How could anyone take her seriously after that? Most of them seemed to have taken it as a joke but Tom had been deadly serious. For months he couldn't get a hard-on unless they could pretend he was one of his mates. It was bizarre. For a while she thought he might be a homosexual, so obsessed was he by the size of his own and other men's penises. But it was nothing like that. These guys were just normal and could still get pleasure out of fucking the person they loved. She never let herself forget the fact that all men were not like Tom.

The mangled, saliva-tasting bogey of pork finally went down. It was probably out of this world but she couldn't taste anything. Little snippets of nonsense that Tom was coming out with kept piercing her reverie and making her wince.

'So how many women do you get through at an average party? Do the guys ever get a bit, you know, amorous with each other, haw haw haw haw . . . oh Stewart, that sounds absolutely amazing.'

She couldn't bear another second of this shit. She couldn't bear the thought that they might think she was remotely impressed by any of this crap. Suddenly she was standing up without actually being able to remember the physical movement of having got there. They all went deadly silent and gawked at her.

'Erm, em . . . I'm just popping to the loo.'

Tom and Liz both stood up to escort her but she insisted they sit down.

'No, please, it's OK. I'm fine. I just want to be on my own for a minute.'

Liz looked genuinely concerned. Tom just looked pissed off. Clutching her bag, Christine shuffled off towards the ladies'. Tom let out a loud guffaw as she walked away from the dining area and for a moment she could think of not one good reason why they stayed together. Walking past the toilets, through reception and out into the car park the cold, fumy night air of the Barnton roundabout enlivened her. The noise of the traffic gave her a feeling of being a small part of something very big. The sound of hundreds of different people, none of them probably as bad as the three arseholes she'd just left in the restaurant, was reassuring.

As an elderly couple gittered out of a taxi at the side of the road, Christine pictured them in spiked bras and rubber masks and wondered if they were the next consignment. Impulsively, she found herself clambering over the wall towards them, pulling down her skirt to protect them from her black nylon thrush specials.

She squeezed into the taxi as they argued about whether to give a tip and what would be the most practical way to carry the cases. The taxi driver was glad to get away before he got roped into helping them.

As they whizzed up Drumbrae she lounged back in the seat and exhaled. The sense of freedom was exhilarating. It made her feel really strong.

'Good night out was it, love?' chirped the taxi driver, having noticed her glee in the mirror.

'Absolutely fucking awful!'

His eyes furrowed in reflection and he went quiet as they purred along the twisting road to the estate. Tom and the neighbours hated when she referred to their beloved Baberton thus but that's all it was. It was like Livingston the sequel but for some reason the people who lived there thought it was posh. It was where poor people with no imagination who had made a bit of money went to pretend to be middle-class and die. Hasta la vista, Baberton.

Giving the taxi driver a £1.50 tip she hurried up to the

house. It would be best to take as much as possible now as she didn't want to come back until she was strong enough not to stay. This was it. This was really it this time. She still had to find somewhere to go but she'd pack first, it would be harder to change her mind once everything was ready to go.

Lifting bales of clothes still on their hangers, she humped them into the two cases, then into bin bags along with the contents of her knicker drawer, some tops, jumpers. The dressing table was cleared with one sweep of her arm into a carrier bag. A whiff of mingled perfume wafted from the top as she carried it out to the door with the cases and other bags. It reminded her of their going-out smell but she blocked it from her mind and instead thought about how painful anal sex was with a semi and no lubrication. It was essential just to keep moving. If she wasn't out of there before he came back it would be too late, just like the other times.

Raking through the box file they kept in the living room she pulled out all the official things she might need – passport, driving licence, bank statements, medical card, video card, cheque book and put them in a holdall with some books, toiletries, tapes, walkman, various obscene photos he'd taken of her, along with the customary lot of useless shite she hadn't looked at in years. Finally she threw her filofax on top then slumped down on the settee with the phone on her lap. Sandra wouldn't mind her staying for a few days.

'Hiya, how are you doing? Look, Sandra, I have to ask you a huge favour.'

Sandra uh-huhed apprehensively.

'This is going to sound strange but, look, I'm leaving Tom.'

'Oh no, I'm really sorry, Christine. What's happened?'

'Please, Sandra, I don't have time to explain right now.

I have everything packed. I just can't stand it any more, honestly. Could I possibly use your boxroom? Just for a couple of days till I get something else sorted out?'

Silence.

'Hello? I won't get in the way. I'll keep myself to myself.'

'Christine, I don't know what to say. I'm really sorry for you but Jim's got a couple of high heid yins coming round. We think there could be a promotion on the cards. You know how long he's waited for this. I'm really sorry I have to let you down.'

Christine couldn't believe what she was hearing, couldn't believe the full barrage of pathetic excuses. Tears were coming, she couldn't help it.

'Honestly, Sandra, I'll just sit in the room and read. You won't even know I'm there. I have to get out.'

'Please don't do this, Christine. I hate it when I can't help you out. Don't make me feel any worse about it. Why don't you think about it for a few days? It's awfully sudden for such a big decision.'

'Do you really think I'd do something like this if I wasn't sure? You know me, Sandra. Do you really think I'd do that? Please, I have to get out before he comes back.' She was sobbing now, not in an attempt to emotionally blackmail her friend but because she simply couldn't help it.

'Stop it, please. You know how nervous Jim is with folk at the best of times. It's just not possible. I'm really sorry.'

The bitch. The bloody bitch. After all the times she'd helped her out. Chumming her to the hospital when her dad was dying in St John's. Three hours on buses every fucking night. And going to check on Jim to see if he had a woman in when Sandra had been away at that conference in Aberdeen.

Why did people use her? What was it about her that made people treat her like this?

'Will you give me a ring tomorrow and let me know how you got on?'

As if this was some trivial little thing that would be all right in the morning.

'OK, thanks for nothing. I have to go. I have to find somewhere to go.'

Throwing the phone down she let out a tormented wail, trying to look at the clock through her watery eyes. How long had she been home? Would he leave as soon as he realised she was gone? Would he hell. Leisurely finishing his dinner and arse-licking some more he'd offer to pay and probably have the gall to arrange another date. Surely he wouldn't go through with it without her. What the hell, she'd be gone long before that became apparent.

Still there was no time to waste. Next her friend Su. Su had stayed with them for a couple of weeks when she'd been thrown out her third-last bedsit. Tom and her really didn't hit it off so she was always a good place to go for a slagging session. Su was always guaranteed to reassure her with a lecture on why men who make women wear stockings don't deserve women or her theories on men having invented feminism so women would pretend to like sex a bit more. When things were going well with Tom she generally didn't see Su for months on end because during those times she was just a blemish on something that was fragile but otherwise intact. In this particular instance though, she was probably an even better bet than Sandra.

Su's teenage son answered.

'Hello, Toby, it's Chrissie. Is your mum there?'

'Nut!'

'Do you know when she'll be back?'

'Wnsdie,' he mumbled, then a long pause and 'Shi's it Cath's in Hull.'

Christine wanted to scream. It wasn't Toby's fault however so she retained her composure.

'I hope you're not having wild parties when she's away.'

'Nu-ut!'

She wouldn't bother him any longer. He was at that age where people over the age of seventeen were just embarrassing nuisances who ought to be ashamed of themselves for not having died yet.

'Can you say I'll phone her at the end of the week?'

'Right then,' click, and suddenly she was alone again. Next her old schoolfriend Carol who she hadn't even sent a Christmas card to last year . . . no reply.

Retrieving her filofax from the holdall she started thumbing through it in creeping desperation. Pages and pages of names and addresses of people she'd stopped seeing for no real reason after she'd married Tom. The rest were friends of her family who were either dead or almost dead or college friends who would gladly put her up but all stayed in the south of England. Fuck.

There was no alternative but to try Callum. They'd fallen out with each other about six months ago because she kept arranging to meet him then not turning up, generally because she wanted to stay in and vegetate with Tom. Hanging about on the gay scene had been great when she'd been a teenager but Tom went on about poofs so much she'd sort of gone off them herself. They were so unbelievably selfish. Callum would give her a hard time but what the hell, it was good to talk.

'Callum, it's me.'

'Jesus, Mary and Joseph, if it's not the prodigal fag hag! Where's loverboy tonight then? B&Q?'

'I'm sorry about everything, Callum. I've really missed you. You know the . . .'

'Wait, Dolores, listen, listen.' There was a fumbling and giggling, the sound of the receiver being dropped about on the other end of the line, then a boy's voice.

'Christine. Hi there. I don't know what to say. He's just given the phone to me.'

More fumbling.

'Aye, how about that, eh? Mind that wee bit trade I was chasing, the one at Cheynes? When I was going through my well-coiffured stage? I've been a busy boy in your absence, Dolores. My thigh muscles are like lampposts.'

Christine started to cry again.

'What's wrong? Dinnae get upset, hen, you can still do something with that unsightly cellulite. It's never too late to start exercising.'

'Callum, please listen. I've left Tom. I'm leaving him. I need somewhere to crash for the next couple of days. Just till I get sorted. I can lick your wounds.'

God, it was making her sick to grovel to him.

'Oor man Flint husnae bashed you, has he?'

'No, nothing like that. He's not like that.'

'Ocht, he's no been pishing on you in the bath again has he?'

'Callum, please. I know you're angry with me but I really need to get out of here before he gets back.'

'Ah dinnae ken, hen, you heteros. Why do you no listen to your auntie Callum and find yourself a nice wee dyke?'

Jesus this was heavy going. Fucking men. They were all

as bad as each other, women coming a very close second. He was really making her crawl to him.

'Callum, I'm begging you. I have my worldly belongings in bin bags in the hall. If I don't do it now I promise you I never will. I just need a floor to sleep on for a couple of nights. Maybe just tonight. I know I've got a fucking nerve.'

'Not at all, not at all, hen. I'd really love to have you down and everything but the thing is, me and the boy wonder here are in a heavy cohabiting scene at the moment, know that hibernation for a few months sort of shit? And you know what my wee room's like. There's not enough space to contain our torrents of passion let alone the three of us. I do hate letting you down, Dolores. I'm genuinely awfie sorry, doll. But still leave the bastard. We could all go out to Ce Ce's tomorrow if you're free, free at last.'

A car door banged outside and she heard the sound of his key in the lock.

'Oh fuck. That's him back. Shite!'

Gently placing the receiver down she started to put on her coat. She heard the front door opening and slamming and Tom's voice.

'What the fuck?'

He walked into the living room, his arm still pointing out into the hall with a look of extreme anguish on his face.

'What's going on, babes?'

Christine hung her head, helpless, already weakening towards him.

'Sweetheart, why's all that stuff in the hall? Why did you run off like that? Please, baby, please, what the fuck is this? Please tell me what's going on because I'm starting to get fucking upset here.'

Now he was greeting as well. She had to fight the instinct

to go and comfort him. This was hopeless. If it wasn't for that fucking awful bitch Sandra she'd be gone by now. Then Tom was over with his arms fumbling around her. She tried to pull away but he just squeezed her tighter.

'Don't go, baby, please don't go. Please, please don't leave me, baby.'

It was impossible not to hug him back. He responded to her squeeze with a miserable hoarse little moan, snuggling into her until she could feel his warmth radiating through her clothes.

'I'm sorry I made you go there tonight. I'm a selfish bastard, I know I am, but I'll try. I'll never make you do anything you don't want to again. I just want you, darling. Nothing else matters. I love you, booby joe, I really do.'

And that was all it took. That was all it ever took. How could such an insignificant little man have such a ridiculously powerful effect on her. It was maybe just meant to be, and in all honesty she had nowhere else to go. There was nowhere else she wanted to go now. Things would be better though, now that he was clear about how she felt. Things would be different this time.

I Am Gone

THE ACCIDENT WAS a fortnight ago and I haven't been able to leave her side since. Apart from some new dirty plates on the carpet Sue hasn't moved anything. The flat's exactly as it was when I left that morning. Perhaps by keeping things the way they were she can pretend nothing's happened. She's seen nobody since the funeral and is still acting almost as if she's only just found out. There is solace in her grief though.

Any time in the past I've seen her upset like this I just couldn't handle it. I'd get so wound up I'd have to lock myself in the spare room till she calmed down. Over the past two weeks though I've studied every tear, relishing them almost. If she doesn't cry for a while I start to worry she's getting over it. Before, her hysterics would have driven me out the door, now, I thrive on them. They justify me being here. They are all that justifies me being here.

Each night I sit on the end of Sue's bed and watch her sleep. I can recall everything we ever did together, every taste, smell, touch, stroke, argument, cuddle with total clarity. Just by bringing an incident to mind I can happily replay it in Sensurround as she sleeps.

When she's awake it's even better. All the crappy TV programmes she either wouldn't let me watch or slagged so much I went off them she now views religiously – *Home and Away*, *Blind Date*, *This Morning*. If truth be told though, she still doesn't actually watch them. They are just on at high volume while she gawps at the walls, or sobs over photos and letters whilst devouring packet after packet of Hobnobs.

For the first few days the phone didn't stop ringing. I had to watch her sitting, dumbstruck, listening to all these people who'd been avoiding us for years pretending they were sorry. Even that bastard Grant had the nerve to phone. Sue and I first met just after he dumped her. It was easier to make her see the light when he'd already switched it off. It was during his last call that she pulled the phone out the wall, much to my delight. She only plugged it back in last night.

I'm lying on the bed watching a chink of sunlight through the curtain snowtip the dark mountain of her face. The slow crescendo of the bus engines outside heralds the morning rush hour but the room retains its silence. I'm back to the day I put the note in Sue's drawer at college. When she went out shopping and didn't come back to the halls of residence till nine that night. Then she came to my room and started giving me all that just-want-you-as-a-friend, don't-talk-about-it-it-makes-me-uncomfortable rubbish. Her hair was pulled up in a band and she had on her Aran cardigan and Cockburn Street Market hippy skirt. There was that strong smell of Shalimar that seemed to pervade everywhere she went. For an hour I let her try and talk her way out of my life, then I just started necking her. She loved it, just like I'd told her she would.

I'm getting to the best bit of this glorious thought when the bloody phone starts ringing. It's only 8.45 so it must be her mother. Nobody else would be selfish enough to phone at this ridiculous hour. I watch Sue's face come to life as she fumbles about in confusion then lunges blindly through to the living room. Five sharp yes's, each about a minute apart, then a clutter of OKs, two numbers (ten and thirty), and a couple of whining rights and I sense that we are going to see her mother this morning.

Sue rather thoughtfully switches on the TV before skulking off to the bathroom. I decide I'll just watch a bit of *Chain Letters* till she switches on the taps then I'll go and watch her wash. The taps aren't switched on though. Instead I hear several thunderous farts followed by such a seeming volume of skitters I fear she'll need a plumber. This comes as a bit of a shock as I've only heard her pass wind once before when she was choked with the flu and bending over for a hanky. That was little more than a sigh in comparison. We never fell into that letting-it-all-out-shows-you're-comfortable-together lark that so many of our friends got into just prior to their sex lives breaking down irretrievably. The toilet was a place we both went to spray air freshener.

My illusion of her remains unshattered. When she emerges from the toilet, still unwashed, not giving a fuck because of me, I forget about it. If only I could speak to her. It's stupid but *Kilroy*'s on the other side and it's annoying not being able to watch it. It's lack of control over stupid little things like this that are irritating, like they were the most important things about being alive.

As I sit on the bunker watching her make a cup of tea I notice a photo of us on the fridge. The one outside the hostel in Amsterdam with the guy that wore the nappy with the teddy-bear and dummy. Where did she dig that up? We went there for a week about three years ago but had to come back after two days because we were so paranoid. I'm so touched she's put the photo there though, it sort of makes me realise she really did love me.

As she finishes her tea and starts climbing into her trainers I begin worrying about seeing her mother. Mrs Todd never acknowledged we were a couple. She was forever trying to fix Sue up with one man or another in front of me. She probably hoped I'd just disappear. There's no way out of it now though. If I don't go wherever Sue goes that'll be it, that's the deal. It's probably some kind of test to discover just how inseparable we really are. A morning with her mother will certainly be that.

As Sue opens the door to the flat, the neighbour is loitering with intent outside as if she's maybe been waiting there several days.

'I was awfie vexed to hear about your friend, dear.'

'Thanks Mrs Anderson,' mumbles Sue, trying to squeeze past her.

Old hypocrite. It was she who informed the whole stair we were a couple. Not that I minded anybody knowing but she must have been listening to us through the wall. There's no other way she could have known. It's not as if we walked about in combat gear and when we had sex it was always embarrassingly quiet. She must have been earwigging twenty-four hours a day.

The old vulture blocks the way, wanting some further scraps of information to regale the rest of the neighbours with; an exclusive of some sort.

'It said in the paper she didn't suffer. That must be a comfort to you.'

Sue is still trying to escape, flustered by her sudden false concern.

'Is that what you want to hear? That doesn't comfort me in the slightest, you know?'

As the neighbour's jaw drops, Sue pushes past and makes her getaway. I'm so pleased with her. As I follow, I punch the old cow in the tit but sadly she doesn't notice.

We walk down through the Links. Being invisible is cool as

I could walk about with my finger up my nose and a splayed beaver and nobody would notice. I've never felt so safe. My only concern is that we get separated somehow because I know if I lose her that'll be it. Since there's only people walking dogs and a few students cagily sunbathing around a joint this doesn't seem likely. I'm slightly annoyed that I can't go into our favourite baker and buy a box of gorgeous french pastries – but annoyed in a Prozacked, what-the-fuck sort of way.

Sue stops to look in the baker's window. Is she thinking the same thing? For her too it'll be silly wee things like this that are hardest to take. Her skin looks jaundiced through lack of daylight. I notice a hint of crow's feet cracking beside her eyes, which I'm sure she didn't have before. They make her look even better.

As we walk down past the Methodist shop I get this strange feeling that I'm being watched. I begin checking the faces of the people around us and I realise that every now and again I'm getting a little knowing smile. Some of these people are like me, I sense, but seem to manage holding conversations with their mortal companions, people I thought were just talking to themselves before. We pass about six of them on this one stretch of pavement. How can they communicate? Will I be able to eventually? Just as we cross the road next to Woolworths, Sue suddenly turns and looks right through me.

'What?' she says cautiously, then immediately looks embarrassed and carries on across the road at speed. I run, shouting after her, but either she can't hear me any more or didn't really hear me in the first place.

Surely I'll be able to talk to her soon though, that has to be why I'm lingering like this. She has to know there's more to dying than a banquet for the maggots. I have to tell her I'm waiting, not to worry.

I feel an overwhelming rush of pity for Sue and take her hand. It lies limp in my grasp but I keep holding on to it as we turn into her mother's street. Mrs Todd is so off with me at the best of times I'm worried what she might say about me now I'm out the picture. Surely out of respect, at least till they get the headstone up, she won't be too unpleasant.

When she opens the door I'm taken aback. She looks even more haggard than Sue. Though smartly dressed and clean-looking as usual, her face has a now-familiar magnolia pallor and the undercarriages of her eyes have darkened with worry. The two women embrace tightly for what seems like ages. It looks completely natural but I know it is a first time for them both. Sue was forever complaining about it. That Mrs Todd should finally choose to do it now, about me, in *public*, shocks me to such an extent that I'm soon in tears myself. Stepping towards the huddle I extend an arm towards each of them but they disperse instantaneously and hurry into the house. I only just make it into the hall before the front door is closed. God, that was close. Another second and I'd have lost her.

Sue follows her mother into the kitchen. They're both in tears but struggling to go through the usual motions. Sue is offered and declines tea, coffee, a wee cup of cocoa, a nice biscuit, a little sandwich, a super Lean Cuisine, a bit of last night's stew microwaved, a look at her sister's wedding video, a candlewick for the bed (could this be a final acceptance that we slept together?), a wee drinkie and her old room back before her mother finally starts to wind down. On the way through to the living room Mrs Todd suddenly goes completely gaga, wailing in a really bizarre, uninhibited way, rocking on the spot like Arthur Fowler when he stole the Xmas Club money. Could this possibly be about me? Did this woman actually like me despite everything?

Sue holds her and slowly calms her down. They stand gently exchanging the role of comforter until they have pulled each other together sufficiently to make it through to the settee. I watch them watching each other, not speaking but saying lots. The closer I look the more similar they seem to be, like mirror images.

'The last week's been like a really long, horrible day. Sorry I've not phoned. It's not even hit me yet, properly, you know. I know it's not. I just feel so angry.'

Mrs Todd kisses her daughter's fingers. She's honestly not usually like this, she never has been.

'She'll be watching over you somewhere, dear. I think your dad watches over me. Just light a little candle in your heart for her and keep it burning. She won't go away if you want her there.'

Why was she never like this before? What an absolute dear. I feel like Jimmy Stewart in *It's a Wonderful Life*. It goes on like this for about an hour as I listen on absolutely gobsmacked. She has me in tears about a dozen times with all these brilliant wee anecdotes about things she'd remembered and I hadn't.

By the time we leave, Sue and Mrs Todd are both glowing slightly having seemed to resolve a lifetime of petty squabbles and loose ends. It's sad it takes something so extreme for people to sort things out. When we get to the front door Mrs Todd produces a candlewick bursting out of a Sainsbury's bag.

'You'll need a wee extra something to keep you warm at night now.'

Sue chews at her bottom lip to stop it trembling as she kisses her mum goodbye.

'If you see wee Shona tell her she can come back now. I sent her out to play so we could have a wee while alone together. I'm looking after her for Alison.'

'I will, mum. Look, thanks. You've been great.'

Tears drip off Sue's chin as we walk down the street, leaving her mother standing on the path, huddled alone, looking small and helpless.

It's almost unbearable not being able to discuss how incredibly nice her mother's being about us, finally. And when they cuddled it looked so strange but so normal at the same time. Who can Sue tell about it though? Who'd really understand what a big deal it was except me? Fuck.

We give Mrs Todd's scarecrow silhouette a final wave as we turn into Grove Street. Sue's sister's wee girl is sitting on the pavement, scraping cartoon faces onto the slabs with a stone. She's so in her own little world she doesn't realise there's anyone there.

'Hiya Shona, what're you drawing, you wee vandal?'

As the child looks at Sue, then me, her face takes on an exaggerated expression of fear and confusion. A terrified scream fills the street. Sue's down on her haunches, trying to calm her down.

'What's the matter, Shona? What is it, pal? Has someone hurt you?'

The wee girl wrenches herself away, petrified, and runs round the corner screaming at the top of her lungs, 'Scary man. Scary man.'

Sue's off after the frightened little thing with me in tow. When Shona realises we're behind her it makes her worse. What the fuck am I going to do? I know she can see me. She's never believed I was female. Maybe Sue and me being a couple confused her. My short hair and flat-as-a-pancake chest probably didn't help either. I remember going on a downer when she said to me, the first time we met, *I know you're a man. I can see through your wee mask.* She was only about four at the time but no amount of coaxing has ever managed to convince her otherwise.

Why can't we just go back to the flat? Shona mustn't see me again. She's already probably scarred for life. Sue is right behind as we reach the gate. Shona kicks and bangs at her granny's door, shrieking, trembling, absolutely crapping herself.

Squeezing past a baffled-looking Mrs Todd she escapes up the hall, still screaming about the bad man. Sneaking in behind them I slip behind the curtain in the living room. Eventually mother and daughter manage to coax the child through to find out what the hell is wrong with her.

'Someone must have had a go at her. I turned the corner and she was just sitting there, hysterical, going on about a scary man. It must have just happened.'

The phone is pinged and dialled as Mrs Todd takes control of the situation.

'Billy, it's mum. Get round here as quick as you can. Someone's just tried to snatch Shona. He must still be nearby.'

Sue's brother Billy lives just round in Morrison Street. We used to buy our blow off him and he's as rough as the dog's bollocks. Can this really be happening? I can't even explain, I just have to stand and watch.

They sit Shona down on the settee, facing the chink in the curtain I'm staring through. Mrs Todd tries first.

'Where was the scary man, Shona? You can tell granny. What did he try to do to you?'

Nodding her head wildly she keeps on crying, eyeing Sue with utmost suspicion.

'Aye c'mon, Shona, it'll be OK. Just tell us who it was. Was it someone you know?'

The child can't seem to decide whether to trust Sue or not.

'The scary man was there. He was coming to take me away. Dinnae let him get me, granny, please. Dinnae let him get me.'

The doorbell goes and Mrs Todd lets Billy in. His eyes are wild and watery and he looks ready to kill or maim.

'What's going on? Who was it? I'll kill the bastard. What's he done to her, eh, what's he fucking done to her?'

Sue shrugs at him as he collapses on the floor in front of his beloved niece.

'C'mon, pal. Uncle Billy'll get him for you, dinnae you worry, darling. Just tell me who it was. Was it that dirty old bastard that looks like the Dunblane man at number thirty-three?'

Shona doesn't know what to say.

'You won't get into trouble. You've got to tell us though, we can't let him get you. Did he try and touch you? Did he try and do something dirty to you? The baldy man with the glasses?'

Sue gasps and her eyes bulge slightly.

'Oh God, Billy, I think you're right. She was just outside his door when I found her. He'd probably just let her go.'

'Was it? Was it the bad man?'

'Yes, the bad man, the bad man. Dinnae let him get me,' she keeps repeating.

'Fucking right!' roars Billy and barges out the house.

Poor Mrs Todd is hyperventilating into a cupped hand. Her skin is now the colour of concrete and she keeps muttering to herself, 'It's all my fault. Why did I make her go out?

What was I thinking? What have I done, Susan? What have I done?'

Sue tries to phone her sister at work. They seem to shunt her about for ages before she finally gets through.

'Alison, thank God. You have to come to mum's, there's been a bit of trouble . . . no, no, it's all right now . . . yes, she's fine . . . yes . . . really . . . here . . .' and she beckons to Shona '. . . it's mummy. Come and speak to mummy.'

The child edges over reluctantly and takes the large receiver in her tiny hand.

'Mummy, mummy, the scary man was there. He'd come back to get me.'

Sue quickly retrieves the phone and relays the incident in slightly less alarmist tones before her sister has a nervous breakdown.

Clicking the phone back down she looks at her mother who is still mumbling away to herself with her head in her hands, 'Why did I let her outside? He could have killed her.'

Sue gives her a squeeze. 'Don't worry, mum. The main thing is she's safe now. Alison'll be about an hour. I'll wait till Billy gets back then I'll have to go. I'm not up to a big family crisis at the moment.'

They have another cuddle then Mrs Todd trembles off to make a cup of tea. When she returns the atmosphere of anticipation is so strong that neither of them seem able to even speak. How can this be happening? Shona sits watching *Scooby Doo*, stroking the dachshund draught-excluder's ears. Fifteen minutes pass in this suspended animation till the front door goes and all three seem to levitate off their seats. Billy comes tanking into the room, breathing heavily with a small gash in his cheek, gleaming with sweat.

Mrs Todd notices the blood and starts fussing.

'What happened? Did he attack you as well? What's he done to your face?'

Billy puts his fingers to the wound then checks the blood on his hand.

'The bastard came at me with a pen. Fucking psycho.'

He isn't exactly haemorrhaging but he certainly acts like he is. My God, he's attacked some poor unsuspecting wee man who just twenty minutes ago was probably feeding his budgie and looking forward to the midweek lottery draw.

Mrs Todd's whole body is trembling as she hovers hopelessly beside her son.

'What happened? Did you hit him? Have you hurt him?'

Billy grins proudly down at his freshly grazed knuckles.

'What did he say? Did he admit it? Maybe we should get the police,' suggests Sue, a little timeously.

Billy's eyes widen in disbelief.

'Not now, you cannae. I've sorted the bastard. It's the only way, mum. Emergency justice it's called, there was a thing about it on a programme about Muslims the other night.'

Mrs Todd sits down again, trying to take it all in. 'What did he say? Did he tell you what happened?'

'Of course not. He denied it. Who's going to admit to something like that? I had to start hitting him to stop his lies.' My God, he's almost foaming at the mouth. I want to run round to number thirty-three and check the poor wee man's all right but I can't leave Sue. How can I cause so much trouble when I'm not even here?

Billy is spitting his words out, savouring this moment of glory. What must the poor man have thought? What if he's seriously injured him? What if he's killed the poor bugger? What if I get lumbered with his eternal spirit for being the cause of it all? Shona stares up at her uncle with a look of utter infatuation on her face. Can she even remember what all this is about? Billy gets down on one knee in front of her like Superman before he fell off the horse. 'You're going to be fine now sweetheart. Uncle Billy's scared away the scary man. If he ever even looks at you again tell one of us right away, OK, it's important.'

Shona strokes his scarred cheek. Sue and her mother sit in stunned silence as if it's just starting to sink in. The phone starts ringing and this time all four of them jump.

Mrs Todd answers it with the back of her hand melodramatically brushing her forehead. Listening with a look of dread, she quickly gives a little smile of relief.

'Oh Grant, thank God it's only you . . .'

Grant! Sue looks momentarily startled when she hears the name.

'. . . no, we're just having a bit of a crisis here at the moment . . . no, she's all right. She's here just now . . . yes . . . yes . . . sorry, I forgot to tell her . . . here, I'll let you speak to her . . .'

Sue waves her hands about in front of her, not wanting the phone. Mrs Todd tells her not to be silly and makes her take it. What does that bastard want? What's he phoning her mother for, it's been three years.

Sue reluctantly takes the phone and says his name, then there's a long silence as she listens to him ramble on. What the hell is he saying to her? Hoi, she smiled there, what's she playing at? Come on, here. Pull yourself together, woman.

'Maybe another time Grant. We're really in the middle of something at the moment. Give me a quick tinkle at the flat tonight . . . yes, it's plugged in again,' and there's another little giggle as she puts down the phone.

Give me a quick tinkle? How can she even speak to the guy

after the way he's treated her? How can she be so friendly towards him? And when did he get all pally with her mother? She better not see him, she better not fucking see him!

Billy's gone through to the kitchen to clean his wound with Shona still following him like a limpet. Sue's getting her things together, plumping up the carrier bag which is overstuffed with the candlewick. Mrs Todd is looking a semitone calmer following the distraction of the phone call.

'He's nice, that Grant,' she smiles at Sue with a hopeful look on her face I well remember. What a traitor! What happened to all the candles-in-the-heart stuff?

'You just don't know him well enough, mum.'

'I forgot to tell you he'd been trying to get in touch. He was really worried. He phoned here several times. Seems quite keen?'

'Mum! Not now, please,' and she gets up and puts her coat on. 'I really want to get back. Phone me as soon as you hear anything,' then she points through to the kitchen and whispers, 'He's going to be in the jail the morrow.'

Mrs Todd looks convinced, but tries to be positive none-the-less.

'Not at all, dear. The man can't go to the police after what he's done. I've read what they do to people like him in prison.'

Sue looks impatient.

'If he did do anything, mum. What if it was someone else?'

This is obviously the first time Mrs Todd has contemplated this and she bites at her thumb instensely. Sue squeezes her shoulder.

'Ocht, it probably was, she was right outside his door. We can only wait and see. I hate leaving you but I'm really not up to this, mum. It was only two weeks ago.' Mrs Todd scrunches up her chin in solidarity then shouts to Billy and his number one fan that Sue's leaving.

Running outside I hide behind a car. I'm terrified the wee girl will see me and start up again. They're only about ten feet away at the end of the path. Sue is clutching Shona's hand. As she bends down to give her a kiss, the child grips on to her lapels.

'Auntie Sue. Is Karen really gone now?'

Sue forces a thin-lipped smile.

'I'm afraid so. She's died and she won't be coming back again.'

The wee girl looks aghast.

'What, did Billy kill her?'

All three of them have a little laugh. 'No, silly, her car was in an accident with a big lorry. She's in heaven now though, you don't need to get upset.'

In some cryptic way this seems to satisfy Shona so they say their goodbyes and we leave. Waiting, crouched behind the car until they all go back in the house, I bolt after Sue the instant the door shuts. She seems a little less defeated now, not quite as wounded-looking as she did. The idea that the last hour's excitement has managed to take her mind off me a bit makes me gladsad. She hesitates for a second as we pass number thirty-three, then scurries off towards Tollcross.

My desire to communicate with her is more intense than ever. If Shona could see me so clearly why can't anybody else? Will it be the same with other children? I can't believe I was mistaken for a bloke, even after death. It has seriously dunted that feeling of well-being I was hoping would be eternal.

Watching Sue walk up the street, I feel incredibly protective towards her. No matter how difficult it gets, I have to stay with her, look after her. I have to stifle the creeping resentment I'm beginning to feel about her having a whole separate life without me.

Damn it. She's cutting up Grove Street which means we won't pass that section of pavement again. Running ahead I gesture pointlessly, try to bar her way, make her turn around. She blusters onwards in ignorance, snorting loudly in the empty street. Then there's a loud gargle at the back of her throat. Casting a wary eye around her she lobs phlegm into the gutter and continues with a demure Sunday school smile. I'm still too busy trying to entice her round to the Twilight Zone to try and speak to her to worry about how gross this is. 'Oh come on, Sue, I can't go there without you,' I scream at her but she cuts behind the Cameo and I just have to follow her, shaking with frustration.

As she dawdles across Home Street in a dream, a van swerves to avoid her. The driver glowers through the window, beeping so excessively that Sue gets a terrible fright and almost stumbles in front of a bus. I feel guiltily disappointed when she eventually makes it safely to the other side.

She buys two bottles of Chardonnay and sixty Silk Cut in the off licence, which pleases me. Sue stopped smoking six months ago so it suggests she's cracking under the strain. It sounds selfish but how else do I know she really wants me here?

As we cut up Melville Drive I hear children's voices. A man is pushing two young girls on the swings, they are screaming to go higher. Instinctively I worry about them seeing me, then I start to think it would probably be better if they did. Give Sue some sense that I might be here. Surely that would be better than having another helpless pensioner battered senseless. As we approach them I wave my arms, jumping up and down,

'Hello, hello, over there . . .' The two wee girls are too engrossed in their quests to go higher to notice. Just as we pass though, one of them glances at me briefly but seems decidedly uninterested and is soon concentrating on the swing again. Maybe I just look perfectly normal to them, because they don't know me. I give up.

When we get home it feels so safe. Sue leans back on the door to close it and gazes along the hall into the living room. She looks almost apprehensive to go in, like she'd forgotten until now. How can I let her know I'm here, not to give up? Eventually she grudgingly throws her jacket on the hall carpet and goes through to the kitchen to open the wine. Drinking alone was never her forte, it makes her maudlin. Maybe she's planning on getting deliberately lachrymose to punish herself for not thinking about me for a while. Can't it just be natural? Going through to the living room with the bottle, she puts our Suzanne Vega tape on. Oh God, she's really having to force it, I know she is. A few gulps of wine and a puff of Silk Cut is all it takes to get her howling again. Her sorrow is so obviously genuine I feel rotten for thinking she had to bring it on manually. It's such a painful, heartbreaking noise she's making. If only there was some way I could let her know I was with her. Push a penny up a door or something. Isn't that what they do? Kneeling at her feet I put my head on her lap and tell her I love her over and over again. She forces back the wine, lighting up cigarettes, taking a few puffs then stubbing them out. She still does that. It used to drive me mad.

As I sit there, singing along to the tape I gradually feel the alcohol starting to relax her tensed up little body. This is nice. This I can handle. If she could just stay in for the rest of her life things would be fine. But the phone rings and Sue's face takes on that other-worldly look again. I know immediately it's Mrs Todd as the word *police* is included in Sue's opening sentence. It doesn't sound like Billy's been locked up yet but most of her side of the conversation is limited to uh huhs and well-keep-me-posteds. Surely they'll lock him up over this one. We all know he's going to end up there eventually. It's just a matter of when. I ask you, beating the crap out a helpless old man, what a macho arsehole!

Sue is still trying to wind down the conversation with her mother when the doorbell goes. Who the hell is this now? Surely not Alison and the wee girl, God no. Maybe she's come round to pay her last respects and get the truth out of Sue about this scary man. I dive through to the bedroom and hide under the bed as Sue says her goodbyes to her mother. I'll be safe here till I decide how to play this. Then I hear the door open and a male voice, not Billy though. 'Grant!' Sue exclaims. As do I. What the fuck is he doing here?

'What's going on, Sue? I've been up to ninety since I spoke to you, what's happened?'

I'm up from under the bed and in the hall beside them to see what sort of a fight she puts up to keep him out. By the time I get there he's already barged in and walking towards the living room. Sue follows him helplessly, gesturing towards the door, in other words she puts up no real fight whatsoever.

This is the first time I've ever seen the bastard in the flesh. It strikes me how unattractive he is. After all the shit Sue put up with I thought he might at least be reasonably dishy but he's gruesome, like Lyle Lovett only uglier. He pushes his way into the living room and throws himself down on the couch like they've been married for years.

'Grant, please. I don't want to see you. I would have answered the phone if I'd wanted to. Please go.'

Plug doesn't listen to a word.

'Look, tell me what's going on. I've just been round to your mum's and she wouldn't tell me. I thought you'd tried to top yourself.'

'Charming!'

'Naw, you know what I mean. With the Karen thing and that. I know how much you loved her.'

Oh no, not him now.

'I thought you didn't believe it. I thought you thought I just did it to try and turn you on.'

'Dinnae. I understand, I know you think I don't but I do. What's happened though, tell me, Sue. Your old dear's in a right state.'

Sue's still standing in front of him gesturing towards the door.

'Please, Grant, honestly. I've had enough today. I can't handle being with you, I don't want to have to handle it.'

Grant fumbles inside his jacket and proffers a half bottle of Grouse, trying to look boyish and failing by about forty years.

'Let's just have a little drink. I just want to know you're all right, I've been worried about you. I have,' and he pauses to ponder what a wonderfully sensitive guy he is. I stare intently at the glass ashtray, willing it to jump off the table and bang him in the mouth. Get rid of him, Sue, get rid of the bastard!

'I can't, Grant. I just can't,' she says flatly, already exhausted by her own protests.

'Just one tiny drink. Just to put my mind at rest, please, for me. I won't molest you, honest.'

Sue stomps over to the unit, yanks it open and pulls out two glasses.

'There!' she snaps, slamming them down on the coffee table in front of him.

He pats the cushion on the settee beside him.

'Come and sit here. Don't be silly, love.'

My heart is going 190 to the dozen. How could she? How could she let this happen? He'll think he's on a promise now, dirty fucking bastard.

Sue edges into the far corner of the settee, legs clenched with hands squeezed tightly between them, as far from him as possible. I sit down on the floor on the other side of the coffee table. What can I do? Even if he grabs her I won't be able to do anything. Grant hands her a huge measure and they clink glasses. He stares into her eyes, bottom lip out, slimy as fuck.

'Are you still my pal? Eh? You dinnae hate me, do you?'

Sue tries to avoid his helpless puppy look and stares into her drink.

'Are you? Are you still my pal?' and he touches the side of her chin, trying to get her to look at him, so he can try and hypnotise her with his smarm. I bang his glass but it doesn't budge. I punch the bastard in the face but he just continues looming towards her.

'You know I am, Grant. I just can't see you any more. It's nothing to do with Karen, it's me. I'm just not strong enough.'

'God, Sue, nobody's expecting you to be strong at the moment. It'll take time.'

'Not that kind of strong. You don't understand,' and she puts the glass down. 'Really, Grant. You should go before it's too late.'

'What? Are you going to axe me? What do you mean, before it's too late? Before you give in to me, is that what you mean?'

Crawling under the table, I try to knock it over on them.

Then I just go on a spree, sweeping my arm along the cluttered fireplace, kicking things, but especially kicking that bastard.

'I don't know. I don't know what I mean. A fortnight ago I was sitting here with Karen, you know. Now she's gone and I'm sitting here with you. She'll be turning in her grave, she hated you.'

'I never even met the woman.'

'She knew what you were like. She was the only person I told.'

'What I was like, what I was like! I've changed, I told you.'

'Don't, Grant. Karen was so pleased. She really thought she'd made me see the light. Now look at us. She'd be horrified.'

He still hasn't budged but at least she's standing up to him. Just get him out now, tell the bastard you'll call the police if he won't go. What if I have a breakdown with all this? Do they have lithium on this side?

'We're not doing anything wrong. You shouldn't feel guilty about it.'

'But I can't help it.'

'If she really loved you she wouldn't want you to feel unhappy like this, don't you think?'

'She'd want me to grieve for her though, not just splash some water on my face and forget it ever happened.'

'I'm not going to tell you what to think, Sue. You have to deal with it your own way, I'm not going to lecture you. If you want to talk to me then you can, if you don't then you know I'm here if you change your mind. I'm not going to force anything. If you just want me as a friend, that's OK. I missed you, that's all. I'm worried about you. I'm really really sorry about Karen and everything, I know the pair of you had something . . .'

'Grant?'

He looks relieved his crawling has been curtailed as his vocabulary of concern was no doubt almost depleted. When their eyes meet she looks down, ashamed, at her lap.

'What, what is it?'

'Will you hold me?'

My only solace is in the stiff, awkwardness of their initial embrace but then it just seems to go on and on and she's rubbing her arms up and down his back and his foul face is polluting her hair and whispering sweet somethings in her ear. OK, Sue, enough's enough. You've had plenty cuddles for one day. Stop it, just stop it. She's letting out this low, moaning sound but I don't see any tears. Then suddenly they're fucking kissing. Did she kiss him first? I'm sure she did. She did.

Jackets and blouses are sweeping onto the floor. Belt buckles are rattling. It's happening about four feet away from me but I'm not really taking it in. This is just not happening. His arse is bared now, right in front of me, four feet away, so close I can almost smell it, but I can't, I can't really. This is not happening. He's trying to get it into her, muttering obscenities in a horrible growly gremlin-type voice. Sue's grabbing at him like she can't wait, panting out his name like something out of one of the porn films he probably watches. Sue is grunting her head off as Grant's buttocks jab between her thighs. 'Cunt, cunt, right up your fucking cunt, aw baby, aw baby, fucking baby.' The most hellish sounds imaginable and so loud, so fucking loud.

There was a Soldier . . .

HE WATCHED ON the news the burnt-out shell of a house where a Bosnian family lay cremated in their beds. He tried desperately to warm up. The gas canister in the heater was almost empty so the flame remained lit for a decreasing interval each time it was re-ignited. Eventually he gave up, switched off the TV and walked through to the bedroom. It was even colder in there.

It was only seven o'clock but they had an early start in the morning so he set the alarm. His breath vaporised in front of him as he exhaled. It smelt pretty bad in there too. A damp, decaying sort of stench like the bag from the fruit shop that time forgot. He generally liked the cold. It made him feel hardy and Scottish but the smell of dampness gave the impression he was living in a cave.

He sat on the side of the bed and kissed the girl on the cheek. The tip of her nose was freezing. He smiled and got in beside her. They were both fully dressed. It was too cold to contemplate any form of nudity and it would save them time in the morning.

Crawling beneath the downie, he nuzzled up to her. Despite being fully clothed he could still feel a chill from within her cardigan. Unfastening a few buttons at the top of her blouse, he began kissing and biting at her neck. There was a sickly, acrid smell from her that he loved as it reminded him of the girl in Belize in 1990. He burrowed beneath the quilt and slid her knickers off, biting at her legs and the inside of her thighs. Again, that cloying stench and the strong, dirty smell of his cum from the last few days. He stuck his fingers into her. The entrance was cold and dry but inside she was clammy from their fuck a few hours before. The baseness of it all drove him wild and as he continued poking at her he unzipped and released his erection, spitting on his hand to lubricate it. Pulling his slimy fingers out of her and moving them round to locate her arsehole, he began to attempt entry. The sphincter was unyielding. He snarled, pushing emphatically, trying to force in until he finally felt her succumb. As he slid in she let out a throaty gurgle. Staring at her, he stuck his tongue into her gaping mouth, mimicking his sexual movements. She tasted strong and salty. The tightness around his cock was glorious. He loved women who kept still in bed. He hated these bints who could make their pussies speak. Who threw him about the place so he came too quickly and then complained about it. He grunted into her mouth as he climaxed. It had been wonderful to shoot it deep into a woman again. Better still up her arse.

Falling to the side, his head against her shoulder, he listened to her fart in appreciation. The compliant little thing! Why couldn't they all be like this? He nuzzled up to her until her smell anaesthetised him into sleep.

The alarm woke him at quarter to four. Jumping out of bed he jogged through to the kitchen, hugging himself, trying to warm up. It was still dark outside, but it had kept dry overnight.

He prepared a huge breakfast and thawed out by the cooker as the fat sizzled before him. It would be best to eat a lot now as he didn't know how long their journey would take. They couldn't afford to stop for snacks along the way.

He checked the boot of the Escort then took her out to the car and drove slowly out the lane, only accelerating when he reached the main road. The streets were deserted, save for the occasional lone driver. Taking her hand, he smiled at her. He'd be sorry to say goodbye but relationships such as theirs were always short-lived.

He drove out of town, through Hallyburton Forest (an appropriate spot but too close to home) and beyond. From Strathmore to Strathtay, onto the A9 and upwards. The Grampian mountains loomed ominously above them like ferocious painful bruises on the skyline. He drove on. The first sign of day began to light up behind the clouds. He was doing a steady seventy. The motorway bypassed the little Highland villages that he'd spent holidays in as a child – Dalwhinnie, Kingussie, Aviemore. Aviemore had been his favourite as he'd gone there with the school.

Just before seven o'clock they reached the forest. A dense, black bastard of a forest. He slowed down as they drove along its border. There was a high fence but he knew there was a gate a few hundred yards along the road.

When the headlights located it he stopped the car and got out to investigate. He hadn't been there for years but remembered there being a path behind it. Opening the gate he drove the car onto the dirt track then closed it again.

He looked at the girl in the front seat. She looked peaceful and content despite everything. There was nothing unusual about catching forty winks in the middle of a long drive. Anyway, they weren't going to get caught. He remembered how terrified he was that first time in 1990 but it had gone like clockwork.

Despite his anxieties he realised he loved this part of it just as much as the rest. Fear of getting caught made him feel larger than life and it was this bravado that had made him put her in the front seat in the first place. Stroking her thigh, it felt like a piece of frozen meat. The thought made him laugh.

They drove along the path. Although the sky had lightened up substantially, branches overhead made it almost impossible to see at some points. He drove very slowly, cursing to himself as the forest became increasingly dense.

After driving for about five minutes they came to a clearing. There were a couple of picnic tables and a small burn ran along at the side. He continued driving. Perhaps there was a house nearby, or worse still a camping site but soon he was into thick undergrowth again. Reversing back to the picnic area, he got out the car and peered through the trees, looking for signs of life – nothing! He drove back onto the path in the direction of the road then stopped. This would do.

He looked at her. Her eyes were closed. The blood around her mouth had long since dried. He took her wisdom tooth out the pocket of his jeans. It fascinated him. The root was about three times the size of the part that was usually visible. It had one of these new white fillings in it. He'd only keep this one though. The rest he could dispose of in the opportune depths of Loch Ness on his way back.

It had seemed silent only minutes before but now the sound of the dawn chorus was almost deafening. Still, this spot seemed fairly secluded – at this time of the morning anyway. He got out the car and opened the passenger door. The sickly smell hit him again as the fresh air made contact with the body. She'd have smelt a lot worse though, if he hadn't kept her in that cold bedroom. He could clean the car this afternoon and get rid of the stink.

Grabbing her under the armpits from the front, he pulled her out. She seemed heavier than she had four days ago when he'd lifted her onto the bed. He dragged her across to the far side of the picnic area, beside the burn, and dropped her onto the gravel. In the daylight her face looked bloated and slightly grotesque and there was quite heavy marking around her throat which he hadn't noticed before. But he'd shagged worse.

Kneeling on the gravel he tore at her blouse. It was hard to rip the cotton hem so he slashed it several times with his penknife then tore it into broad strips that he laid beside her. He walked over to the car and brought a large can of petrol from the boot. Returning to her side, he stared down again at that perfect, soft hole he'd made in her face. The front teeth had come out easily with a hammer but he'd needed pliers for a few at the back. He hadn't done this until the second day though, by which time the gums had started to recede. This had made his job all the easier. He'd done her a favour though. Taking away her identity while simultaneously assuring she gave one of the best blow-jobs on the east coast. It was tempting to have one last shot at her but time was too short to tamper with the evidence anymore.

Rolling her onto her stomach he lifted up her skirt. The knickers must still be on the bed but he'd dispose of them with the sheets when he got back. He inserted the nozzle from the petrol can into her rectum as far as it would go and began pouring until it overflowed. The process was then repeated into her vagina. He doused the rags and stuffed them into each hole as securely as he could, leaving an end dangling out of each to ignite.

Then, turning her over, he did the same to her sucking mouth. When the petrol began pouring down her nostrils, he jammed her facial cavities with the remainder of the cotton. The rest of the can he poured onto her body, and clothing and hair until it was empty. He loved the smell of petrol. It reminded him of filling the articulated trucks in Belize, high on Guatemalan grass with the Central American sun blazing down at him.

Taking the can back to the car, he threw it into the boot then picked up a branch that was lying by the burn. Rolling the girl onto her side he kicked the legs apart and lit the two rags in the middle. The whole of the lower part of her body ignited simultaneously. Jumping up, he held the lighter against the rag hanging from her mouth then walked backwards towards the car, brushing away his footprints with the branch.

By the time he reached the Escort she was blazing gloriously. The stench filled his nostrils and he inhaled deeply. It was a familiar and evocative smell that he'd no doubt encounter again soon as he was on tour with a battalion in Londonderry at the end of the month.

It was hard to take his eyes off her as she slowly disintegrated amidst the flame. The black smoke and sizzling and spitting of fat would attract attention soon though, so he threw the branch in the back of the car, got in and sped off back down the path.

It was completely light now so he could drive quickly plus he felt elated so speeding helped him express this. It only took five minutes to get back onto the country road again. Opening the gate, he cast a final glance down the path then turned left, back the way he'd come.

As he drove away he watched in the wing mirror as faint

hues of smoke began to appear above the trees. He kept to a steady sixty now that he was back on the main road, fearful of drawing attention to himself. He surveyed the reflection of the forest intermittently until it disappeared from sight then drove onwards back to civilisation. As he waited at the junction to get back onto the motorway he glanced across at a signpost for Culloden Moor. He smiled to himself. What better resting place for the victim of a Scottish soldier?

 Started in 1992 by **Kevin Williamson**, with help from established young authors **Duncan McLean** and **Gordon Legge**, Rebel Inc magazine set out with the intention of promoting and publishing what was seen then as a new wave of young urban Scottish writers who were kicking back against the literary mainstream.

The Rebel Inc imprint is a development of the magazine ethos, publishing accessible as well as challenging texts aimed at extending the domain of counter-culture literature.

Rebel Inc Fiction

Children of Albion Rovers £5.99 pbk
Welsh, Warner, Legge, Meek, Hird, Reekie
'a fistful of Caledonian classics' **Loaded**

Rovers Return £8.99 pbk
Bourdain, King, Martin, Meek, Hird, Legge
'Pacy, punchy, state of the era' **iD**

Beam Me Up, Scotty Michael Guinzburg £6.99 pbk
'Riveting to the last page...Violent, funny and furious.' **The Observer**

Fup Jim Dodge £7.99 hbk
'an extraordinary little book ... as good as writing gets' **Literary Review**

Nail and Other Stories Laura Hird £6.99 pbk
'confirms the flowering of a wonderfully versatile imagination on the literary horizon' **Independent on Sunday**

Kill Kill Faster Faster Joel Rose £6.99 pbk
'A modern urban masterpiece' **Irvine Welsh**

The Sinaloa Story Barry Gifford £8.99 pbk
'Gifford cuts through to the heart of what makes a good novel readable and entertaining' **Elmore Leonard**

The Wild Life of Sailor and Lula Barry Gifford £9.99 pbk
'Gifford is all the proof that the world will ever need that a writer who listens with his heart is capable of telling anyone's story.' **Armistead Maupin**

My Brother's Gun Ray Loriga £6.99 pbk
'A fascinating cross between Marguerite Duras and Jim Thompson'
Pedro Almodovar

Rebel Inc Non-Fiction

A Life in Pieces Campbell / Niel £10.99 pbk
'Trocchi's self-fragmented lives and works are graphically recalled in this sensitively orchestrated miscellany.' **The Sunday Times**

The Drinkers' Guide to the Middle East Will Lawson £5.99 pbk
'Acerbic and opinionated .. it provides a surprisingly perceptive and practical guide for travellers who want to live a little without causing a diplomatic incident.' **The Guardian**

Locked in the Arms of a Crazy Life: A Biography of Charles Bukowski Howard Sounes £16.99 hbk
'wonderful...this is the first serious and thorough Bukowski biography. An excellent book about a remarkable man.' **Time Out**

Drugs and the Party Line Kevin Williamson £5.99 pbk
'essential reading for Blair, his Czar, and the rest of us' **The Face**

Rebel Inc Classics

Snowblind Robert Sabbag £6.99pbk
with an introduction by Howard Marks
'A flat-out ballbuster. It moves like a threshing machine with a full tank of ether. This guy Sabbag is a whip-song writer.' **Hunter S. Thompson**

Stone Junction Jim Dodge £6.99 pbk
with an introduction by Thomas Pynchon
'Reading *Stone Junction* is like being at a non-stop party in celebration of everything that matters.' **Thomas Pynchon**

Hunger Knut Hamsun £6.99 pbk
with an introduction by Duncan McLean
'*Hunger* is the crux of Hamsun's claims to mastery. This is the classic novel of humiliation, even beyond Dostoevsky.' **George Steiner** in **The Observer**

Young Adam Alexander Trocchi £6.99 pbk
'Everyone should read *Young Adam*' **TLS**

The Star Rover Jack London £6.99pbk
with introductions by Hugh Collins and T. C. Campbell
'an astonishing achievement' **The Sunday Times**

A Walk on the Wild Side Nelson Algren £6.99pbk
with an introduction by Russell Banks
'Mr Algren, boy you are good.' **Ernest Hemingway**

Rebel Inc. Classics

Revenge of the Lawn Richard Brautigan £6.99 pbk
'His style and wit transmit so much energy that energy itself becomes the message. Brautigan makes all the senses breathe. Only a hedonist could cram so much life onto a single page.' **Newsweek**

The Blind Owl Sadegh Hedayat £6.99 pbk
with an introduction by Alan Warner
'One of the most extraordinary books I've ever read. Chilling and beautiful'
The Guardian

Helen & Desire Alexander Trocchi £6.99 pbk
with an introduction by Edwin Morgan
'a spicily pornographic tale ... enhanced by an elegant and intelligent introduction' **The Scotsman**

Sombrero Fallout Richard Brautigan £6.99 pbk
'Playful and serious, hilarious and melacholy, profound and absurd ... how delightfully unique a prose writer Brautigan is.' **TLS**

The Man with the Golden Arm Nelson Algren £7.99 pbk
'This is a man writing and you should not read it if you cannot take a punch ... Mr Algren can hit with both hands and move around and he will kill you if you are not awfully careful.' **Ernest Hemingway**

Ask the Dust John Fante £6.99 pbk
with an introduction by Charles Bukowski
'a tough and beautifully realised tale...affecting, powerful and poignant stuff'
Time Out

Not Fade Away Jim Dodge £6.99pbk
'a book which screams off the starting blocks and just keeps accelerating'
Uncut Magazine

All of the above titles are available in good bookshops,
or can be ordered directly from:
Canongate Books, 14 High Street, Edinburgh EH1 1TE
Tel 0131 557 5111 Fax 0131 557 5211
email info@canongate.co.uk
http://www.canongate.co.uk